ALSO BY TREVOR TUCKER

Ned Kelly's Son

A saga of Australian heritage ... almost lost in history.

The Stolen Maps

Australia's greatest maritime secret?

Aussie Anecdotes

A collection of quintessential Australian short stories.

A Sense of Justice

A tale of retribution for two unlikely Australian heroes.

God only knows when.

A look at the criminal underbelly of rural Australia and the consequences of farm invasion and stock theft.

Wonnangatta.

A sweeping saga of mystery, murder, romance and intrigue played out against the raw beauty of the Australian bush.

THE DIAMOND WHISPERER

TREVOR TUCKER

TREVOR TUCKER PUBLISHING

To my amazing grandchildren Tylah and Jesse Ryder.

1

I'm an old bastard now, and live alone, but I'm not immune from being drawn to the luxuries of life, particularly those which, for various reasons, have eluded me too easily.

That's why I'm now holidaying in Victoria's high country at Dinner Plain, a small, secluded alpine village located close to Mount Hotham, one of Victoria's most glamorous and outrageously expensive ski resorts; but that's not for me.

It's amazing how beautiful this place is. A few minutes ago, I wiped away a film of condensation from the inside surface of the lounge room windows. That small task enabled me to then witness thick clouds being pushed along at a high rate of knots by the wind to reveal not only deep valleys nearby, but the spectacle of row upon row of distant mountain ranges covered in snow for as far as I could see in just about every direction.

Currently, I'm lounging contentedly in an old armchair, in front of a cheerful fire, sipping a fabulous Mount Moornapa shiraz and absorbed in a novel: *Ned Kelly's Son*. I never thought Ned had a son, but I was wrong, so it turns out. It's compelling reading; a glimpse into rural life after early Australian colonization, and of the subsequent lives of our lesser-known pioneers (heroes all).

It's nice to be able to put that book aside occasionally and listen to the snowstorm raging outdoors. Last time I checked it was minus ten degrees centigrade outside and a cozy twenty-two degrees centigrade inside. And, earlier this morning a concerned neighbour warned me that the wind was likely to exceed one hundred kilometers per hour at times throughout the day. I had no reason to doubt that forecast when my small chalet suddenly shuddered alarmingly from a particularly powerful blast of wind.

Regardless, in such contrasting circumstances, it's still so easy to remain immersed in one's thoughts and emotions; you know, things like appreciating being free of domestic demands, evolving future travel plans, do I need to buy a new Nissan Pathfinder, should I continue with scuba diving lessons, and contemplating one's regrets.

'What regrets, for Christ's sake!?' I thought, admonishing myself. *'Relax man, you're now safe and free of any dormant consequences. Just relax.'* But hang on! That's easier said than done: why was someone now pounding on the front door of my chalet? I was about to open it but hesitated, my instincts suddenly in overdrive. 'Who's there?' I called.

'A friend. Are you mister Harper, Les Harper?'

'Who wants to know?'

'The Australian Federal Police.'

'So, what's your name, ID and the nature of your enquiry?'

'Be assured it's in your best interests to cooperate, sir. However, I'm not compelled to tell you anything further until you answer my question. Are you Mr. Harper?'

'OK. Yes, I'm Les Harper, so would you now please answer my questions.'

'You've recently come to our attention in relation to some fraudulent dealings perpetrated several years ago. We believe your life is under threat if our latest intelligence proves to be correct. My name's Clam, and my ID is classified information. And right now, I'm your only real friend.

'C'mon Les, it's frigging freezing out here; how about we continue our conversation inside, eh?'

Reasonably confident this bloke was genuine and no immediate threat to me, I released both locks and opened the door just far enough to appraise my new friend, albeit nevertheless with my right foot firmly positioned behind it to prevent him from unexpectedly attempting to crash the door open.

There was no need to worry, for at arm's length Clam had thrust forward a gloved hand which held a card, the type I'd become familiar with over the years. I was surprised and immediately intrigued, rather than shocked, that before me stood an aboriginal man, perhaps six feet plus tall and probably forty to fifty years old.

His face showed no imminent physical threat, so I stepped aside, opening the door fully while waving for Clam to enter. Before doing so, he pocketed his ID card then brushed off the snow which had accumulated upon his beanie and on the shoulders of his coat. Next, he brushed off the snow from his green canvas navvy sack and then slung it carefully onto his shoulder.

Finally, he picked up the gun case which had been resting vertically against the chalet's front wall then, with an air of self-confidence, walked past me into the chalet.

* * *

'MAKE YOURSELF COMFORTABLE, Clam. I suppose you could do with a brew right now; tea or coffee?'

'Coffee'd be real nice. And then some warm milk for this grey and white beast,' Clam said, smiling as he untied his navvy sack and gently withdrew a tiny, and very sleepy kitten'.

'Where'd you find that?'

'On your front door mat and almost completely covered with snow; thought the poor little bugger would be dead. But not so; and it can't be more than a few weeks old. Anyway, do you mind if I put it on the rug in front of the fire?'

'Good idea. It probably needs to thaw out a tad. I guess it somehow got separated from its mother, or some bastard dumped it.'

The kitten was soon massaging the floor rug and purring loudly, amazingly loud for such a tiny being.

Interestingly, as Clam and I settled into our armchairs, the kitten stretched, yawned, then proceeded to scale the outside of a leg of Clam's trousers. After circling and massaging his crotch, the kitten made itself comfortable and was soon fast asleep, we judged, for the purring stopped abruptly.

Soon after, I hauled myself from my armchair and proceeded to make our coffees. For no reason, I glanced sideways. Clam was removing his beanie to reveal his short, curly and black hair.

'So yes, I'm an Abo. My black face didn't fool you one bit, eh Les?' he said, smiling broadly. 'And I'm proud of it.'

I handed Clam his coffee and said, 'mate, I don't give a rat's arse whether you're black, white or orange, just that we have each other's back.'

'Yeah, I'm good with that. In fact, that's why I'm here. Then I suggest we get started; you can go first to spill yah guts.'

2

———————

A few hours later our kitten stirred. Eyes blinking, it yawned, stretched and then rather rapidly made its way to the hearth in front of the fire where it innocently deposited a neat little turd. Repositioning itself, and while staring contentedly into the near distance, it proceeded to pee unabashedly, not caring who would have to clean up after it of course.

Meowing loudly to obviously grab our undivided attention (as if its life depended on it), Clam set about cleaning up its mess, while I started to warm some milk.

A few minutes later the kitten lost interest in its milk and once again retired to the warmth of the hearth rug.

The snowstorm abated as I was showing Clam to his room, and bugger me, just then someone else had started knocking on the front door.

'Les, it won't be a good idea if I answer the door. I'm not supposed to be here, remember? And my gut feeling says that 4WD now parked out the front is not there just for fun; something stinks.'

I hadn't noticed the vehicle pull up, and Clam was right, its black tinted windows did give it a sinister aura. 'Agreed, I'll answer, but you keep well out of sight.'

'Right, but here, shove this behind your back, just in case, like. I think you already know how to use a Beretta M9.'

I did of course, which gave me a long-forgotten sense of comfort.

'Who's there?' I called.

'It's me, Jennie Czarnecki'.

'What can I do for you, Jennie?

'My kitten has disappeared, and mummy said she thought she saw it on your front veranda just before that nasty storm came along.'

'Well, your mummy was right, I did rescue a kitten just before that storm. So, what colour is your kitten?'

'It's grey and white with a bit of orange in its coat, and it has a long fluffy tail.'

'And its name is ... ?'

'We only decided on Missy a few days ago, and she's soooo beautiful'.

'OK Jennie, have you got something to carry Missy in?'

'Oh yes, this shoe box, and her favourite blanket.'

'Hang on a few seconds, young lady, I'll get her for you.'

I collected Missy and then eased open the front door, albeit with one foot placed firmly behind it, you know, just in case this meeting was a very classy deception.

Before me was the cutest freckle faced girl, a little shy perhaps, no more than five or six years old, beany pulled down over her ears, bubble jacket, thermal jeans and gloves, and ankle high wet weather boots.

'Is this your Missy?'

'Ooohh yes, that's her all right,' she said, smiling and excitedly clapping her hands.

'She's a naughty girl though! No more running away, OK?' Having then lovingly wrapped Missy with the blanket, she gently thrust the kitten into the shoe box.

Jennie then turned, looked at me and said, 'Thanks heaps mister. I'd better get her home now, but I'll see you around, eh?' Instinct told me this wasn't a ruse, and that I wouldn't need the Beretta.

'Yeah probably, but before you skedaddle, is that your mother sitting in the big four-wheel drive out the front there?'

'What four-wheel drive? There's nothing there mister; you must be seeing things.'

She was right. Oooh, how odd, I thought.

'Hang on Jenny, by the sound of your name, were you born in Poland?'

'Yes, I think so; that's what mother told me.'

Smiling, I walked back inside. 'Coast's all clear mate.'

No response: I called again, much louder. 'I hope you're not playing funny buggers because we've still got a lot to talk about.'

Again, nothing!

Somewhat annoyed by Clam's sudden departure, I checked his room. His belongings were there, but the overcoat and boots he'd left to dry by the fire were gone. I shrugged my shoulders and walked back into the kitchen intending to make a cuppa.

About twenty minutes later I heard the chalet's back door being opened then closed ever so quietly.

I need not have worried, for within a few seconds there stood Clam, smiling broadly.

'Well, that was an interesting visitation, I must say,' Clam said while removing his coat and slipping out of his boots.

'You could say that; that young girl was a real beauty, great for a chat, and sharp as a tack. But hang on, where the hell have you been mate?'

'Curiosity got the better of me, so I decided I'd follow that 4 x 4.'

'Did that achieve anything, pray tell?'

'Oh yes, indeed. I followed its tyre tracks and found it about a kilometre from here. Two gentlemen, both of Central European appearance, were about to enter their own chalet.

'They stopped when they saw me approaching but were nowhere as tough as they looked and tried to act.'

'Which means what, exactly?'

'Well, the bloke who drew his gun and aimed it at me is now

dead,' Clam replied without emotion as he placed a handgun on the small table between our armchairs.

'And the other bloke?'

'He's probably going to wake up soon with one hell of a headache … and a chest full of fractured ribs. And, oh yeah, here's his gun, another US Baretta; easily available on the Black-market.

'Neither had any ID, either on them, or openly visible in the chalet. Thought I might have found something more incriminating, had I spent a bit more time going through all their belongings. But no, just these.'

Again, with gloved hands, Clam retrieved a set of car keys from his coat pocket then placed them upon the side table along with the two handguns.

Without further ado, Clam next retrieved a small puck-shaped object from an inside pocket of his coat. 'An electronic tracking device: a transmitter,' he said nonchalantly. 'Found it under your Pathfinder. Perchance *you* didn't put it there?'

'No bloody way!' I replied vehemently. 'Where the bloody hell would I know where to buy something like that? And why would I need it anyway?'

'Please excuse my concern for your safety, but chillout Les and listen. Think about this; it's damn clear to me now that someone with considerable wealth and influence want's you dead.'

'But what have I done to suddenly be on someone's hitlist?'

'Mate, that's what I hope to find out, sooner, rather than later because that tracking device has considerably upped the dangers we're facing.

'I'll arrange for our forensic boys to give this hardware the *once over* for fingerprints. I therefore suggest that once I've finished this cuppa, we pack and then head for the low country, asap like. I need to report to my chief in Canberra.'

'Anything else I should know about?'

'Yep. If you look now in the direction of the Hotham Heights resort, you should probably see a plume of black smoke. That'll be one of their 4 x 4's burning to the ground. At some time, our forensic boys will have a friendly talk with the car rental company and perhaps they'll expose precisely who rented those vehicles.

'Incidentally, I've got photos of both those men on my mobile phone ... which should interest both the AFP, and ASIO. Just ask if you'd like to see those photos, eh Les. Perhaps you'll recognize them.

'We've got great contacts throughout Europe, and those blokes will soon be ID'd if either of them has any form.'

'So, you do work for the AFD; I thought as much.' However, what worried me most at that time was Clam's mirthless reply. 'Correct, but if you ever reveal that to anyone, I'll see to it that your retirement comes to an abrupt end.'

After a quick, but focused "wipe down" of taps, door handles, mugs and cutlery, I left $400.00 on the kitchen table, (to cover my albeit brief stay) then headed outside with my bags to join Clam who already had the rear door of my station wagon open and was loading what looked like the last of his own belongings.

After closing the front door of the chalet, I put its key in the lock, wiped it and the doorknob clean, and then joined Clam who was brushing away heaps of snow which had accumulated on the roof and bonnet of my vehicle.

'I'll drive if you like,' said Clam, not waiting for my approval as he slid behind the wheel.

'She'll be bloody cold, so you'd better sta ...,' was all I got to say, because Clam was already pumping the accelerator and firmly pressing the ignition button. Modern technology prevailed: my Pathfinder 4 x 4 roared into life.

We were only a kilometre down the highway heading for Omeo when my new friend turned to me and said, 'You're right mate, we definitely do need to talk further so let's get a move on.'

3

———

A dense fog accompanied us down to the snow line where Clam pulled off the road and stopped to enable us to remove my snow chains.

That allowed our speed to increase, but almost invisible patches of "black ice" on the road's bitumen surface presented a significant driving hazard for several kilometres. In fact, it wasn't until we arrived at Omeo that normal driving conditions returned.

A good strong coffee was called for, but Clam was in no mood to stop to enjoy it. He relented however when I demanded a toilet stop.

Twenty or so minutes later as we approached the small country town of Swifts Creek, Clam announced the next stage of his plan. 'As luck would have it, a close friend and associate of mine, and his wife, both live here, but they're currently overseas and won't be returning for at least another three weeks. I have their ongoing permission to stay here any time. You're in for a few surprises I'd say.'

At the end of a gravel laneway was a fenced property; by that I mean, a substantial, two-metre-high metal privacy fence wrapped around three sides of the property's boundary. An equally high and substantial metal gate, started to slide open as we pulled up.

I looked at Clam who was now dangling a set of house keys and an electronic door key in front of me. Smiling, he said, 'welcome to our euphemistically named, *Chalet on Tambo*. No photos. OK?'

We drove through the gate then stopped outside a double garage, an integral part of the house, a white, very beautiful colonial inspired creation surrounded by wonderfully maintained lawns and garden beds. And as I was soon to learn, was accompanied by an interior which lacked for nothing.

Immediately, the perimeter gate began to close behind us. Within a few seconds, Clam's mobile phone beeped, apparently as I was soon to learn, indicating the gate was now not only closed, but locked.

'My phone will beep every time the front gate, or the garage door, or any of the house doors or windows are either opened or closed,' said Clam. 'The external surveillance system, which I'll show you later, can also command the gate and house doors to automatically close. It's programmed to not only make it impossible for unwanted intruders to gain access, but to contain them from escaping the house for as long as possible, pretty much the same philosophy used by our Federal Note Printing facility.

'Our boys in Canberra will also receive an immediate alert whenever this security system registers a change in status of any of its sensors. They will also know, right now in fact, that I've accessed this safe house and will have alerted our secret response team. They'll also be monitoring my movements 24/7 until I return to HO. In the meantime, however, should I *drop off their radar* so to speak, my colleagues will immediately start looking for me.'

A single click on Clam's electronic key and the garage door started ascending; when fully open his mobile phone beeped.

After a double click, Clam said, 'the house's indoor security system has now been deactivated so that we can move about without setting off an intruder alarm. But not so with the external system, it remains active 24/7 unless I deactivate or override it.

'Right, let's get unpacked.'

Another two clicks and the garage door descended, and on cue Clam's mobile phone dutifully beeped.

Unpacking in my assigned bedroom only took a minute or two.

Clam, however, was not in the kitchen; I assumed he'd gone to the toilet, so I set about making a cuppa, then searched the fridge for something stronger.

'You'd better sit-down Les, I've got some bad news, 'Clam grimly announced when he suddenly entered the kitchen.'

'Which means *what* exactly?'

'What do you reckon this is?' said Clam, handing me a small puck shaped device.

'It looks a bloody lot like that tracking thingy you removed from under my Pathfinder.'

'And this is a second one. I obviously missed it, which is inexcusable. My sincerest apologies Les; it's standard procedure to double check for multiple tracking bugs, just in case, like.

'This little development changes things significantly. Someone, or some people, are determined to get you; they've gone to a lot of trouble so far ... but for what?'

'Then I suggest we keep talking, because nothing immediately comes to mind. Mate, take a seat on the back veranda while I make a brew ... do you fancy coffee or tea?'

'Coffee, strong, no sugar, thanks Les.'

We settled into very comfortable wicker chairs but said nothing for the first five or so minutes while sipping our coffee's and dunking our biscuits.

'Great view, eh Les? If you're wondering, that's the Tambo River running through the backyard. Apparently, it's never flooded the house, being on this elevated side, but in Spring after the high plains snow starts to melt, it will flood dangerously onto the lower side, and downstream in many places.

'It ends up in the Gippsland Lakes system. And according to some folk I've known most of my life, it was once a fantastic trout fishing stream.'

'That'd make it near impossible to attack the house from that side,' I contributed. 'But why is there no privacy fence along this river side for when there's no flooding?'

'Good point Les, but can you see the four lines of electric fence which span the width of this property?'

'No, but electric fences generally aren't much of a deterrent.'

'They are when they are mains powered. And the beauty of that is that contacting any of them can be lethal. Our fences are designed such that an intruder is likely to be unwittingly in contact with a section of the fence at some stage. The motion detectors sense the intruder's presence, and then immediately apply that lethal voltage.'

'What detectors? I can't see them.'

'If you look carefully Les, you should be able to just make out five carefully placed and cleverly camouflaged boxes hidden in the surrounding shrubbery. Each box houses a high-resolution video camera which connects not only to the kitchen TV, but to my mobile phone. There's also an infrared movement detection sensor within each box which activates the high voltage fence. Look to where I'm pointing Les.'

4

____

We were into our second brew and had barely started our intended serious conversation when Clam kicked my leg under the table and said, 'Not now mate, our talk will need to happen later. We've got unwelcome visitors. I just saw movement on the far side of the paddock directly over the river. Act naturally and don't move until I say ... but be prepared to move bloody fast when I do ... and then follow me.'

'I just saw a small glint of light, like sun reflecting off glass,' I said in a mixed tone of concern and excitement.

'Yep, two blokes only, and if I'm not mistaken that's a dark blue HiLux 4 x 4 ute about ten metres away to their left and behind them. It could possibly be the one I didn't torch. Anyway, that's a pissy weak job at trying to conceal it and themselves. Which means if they're professionals, they seem to be in an awful hurry.

'Regardless, that also means there's been four of those bastards hunting me!'

'So, it would seem. Just so you know Les, about ten minutes ago I got an alarm on my mobile phone that something was parked in our driveway. It was a dark blue HiLux 4 x 4 ute.

'Which means they think we haven't seen them, but then, they're not Abos,' eh Les?

'Bastards, one of them is drawing a bead on us, so get ready to ...' Clam's intended warning was cut short by the zip of a bullet from a high-powered rifle splitting the gap between us and, in what seemed to be in the exact same instant, totally disintegrated a huge earthenware plant-pot sitting on a bench about a metre behind us.

I don't think I'd ever seen anyone move as quick as Clam did in the next second. Before I was able to move, even though I thought my reflexes were still pretty damn sharp, Clam was not only already on the way to the floor but had somehow grabbed my jacket and was hauling me from my seat ... and I was destined for an abrupt hard landing on the tiled floor.

Scrambling on all fours we made it unscathed into the house.

'Grab your stuff, asap like mate', Clam ordered, then added, 'then meet me in the garage. Just throw what you can into the Nissan: no sense trying to neatly pack anything.'

Fortunately, my unpacking on arrival had been minimal, so I only required one trip to the garage. Clam had already thrown his belongings into the Nissan and was in the process of arming the property's external security systems.

'Get in Les and put on your seat belt,' Clam ordered, but quickly added, 'it's my gut feeling our friends will want to inspect this place, but they're in for a bit of a shock ... which should give us a useful head start.'

Seconds later, Clam threw himself behind the Nissan's steering wheel, slammed shut his side door and buckled up. No sooner had he done that, than the garage roller door started to rise, as the front gate began to slide open.

Once outside the fence, Clam stopped the Nissan and commanded the garage door and front gate revert to their closed and secured positions.

'Right, Canberra, here we come,' Clam yelled excitedly as he booted my Nissan forward into an exhilarating charge through the fence gate.

What I didn't realise until later, was that Clam had also already alerted his colleagues in Canberra. Clever things mobile phones: apparently, we were off to meet the cavalry.

* * *

I REFLECTED upon the fast-moving events of the past two days looking for reasons why I was in this situation: nothing obvious surfaced.

We spoke little during the next two hours as Clam concentrated on maintaining every speed limit sign on the Monaro Highway; perhaps he too was assessing things and like me, was looking for a way to safely extract ourselves from harm's way. That silence was not uncomfortable, but rather, relaxing.

About sixty kilometres from Canberra, he suddenly muttered, sounding relieved. 'Arh, there they are, about half a kilometre ahead on the left, just down that side road. See it? That old white Land Rover ute.'

As Clam slowed and turned into that side road, one of the Landy's occupants got out and positioned himself at the rear of the ute. The other bloke remained in the ute though he had slid down so far in his seat that only the top half of his head was visible.

'That's Leigh who just got out, and that's Thommo still in the ute,' Clam said quietly. 'Standard procedure in cases like this; never present a common target, just in case it's the enemy.'

That said, Clam wound down his door window, thrust out his right arm and made an unusual hand signal; something akin to a crocodile opening and closing its jaws.

By the time Clam stopped my Nissan, both men had revealed themselves, one on each side of their Landy. Yet it wasn't until Clam, and I had stepped from the Nissan that they casually holstered their revolvers.

For all intent and purpose, Leigh and Thommo were just a couple of typical Australian farmers. Both wore dusty well-worn RM Williams riding boots, nondescript and stained green trousers, and long sleeve dun-coloured shirts with collars raised. Those shirts were loose fitting to no doubt conceal their guns—and both wore identically styled, wide brimmed Akubra hats.

To further conceal their identity, what better than to have four live sheep and the same number of hay bales in the old ute's carry tray.

As Clam introduced me to these men, I had the opportunity to more closely observe them. Leigh, I guessed was the eldest, probably in his early thirties. Thommo I again guessed, was in his late twenties and stood at least six foot two inches tall, about four inches taller than Leigh.

Their handshakes were very firm, and both had strong athletic builds. Obviously too, neither had shaved for the past few days. Their eyes sparkled confidently and easily held my gaze, their greetings polite and genuinely welcoming.

One other small detail had not gone unnoticed; neither had any dirt under their fingernails.

'If it's OK with you Clam and Les,' said Leigh without further ado, 'I suggest we keep moving. Normal drill, Clam; you lead but stick to the speed limits. Don't want the local boys in blue getting upset and screwing things up for us. We'll overtake you as we get close to Canberra and show you to your digs.

'One more thing Les,' Leigh added quickly, 'Clam will give you a mask to wear before we enter Canberra's suburbs. It's for your safety mate; sure, it'll hide your face, but more importantly we don't want you to know where we are taking you.'

'C'mon fella's, you're going a bit over the top, aren't you?' I replied, sounding far too flippant than which my situation demanded.

'Not if you unfortunately end up in the wrong company,' Thommo said in a serious, reasonable manner. 'To reveal the location of one of our safe houses could be a disaster and result in some of our officers being murdered. Far better that you honestly have no idea where you were accommodated when you're about to lose your balls!'

'OK. I get it. Well, I think I do, but I'm still at a loss about why you blokes are taking so much interest in my wellbeing.'

'All in good time mate,' Clam placated me.

A few minutes later as we said farewell to our escort, Leigh announced what I was waiting for. 'By the way, you blokes have a meeting with the boss tomorrow arvo at two o'clock here, so don't go walkabout. We'll be coming along too, so we'll see you again soon enough.'

'And' said Thommo, just as he was about to get back into the Landy ute, 'perhaps Les can tell everyone why he took particular notice of our clean fingernails but didn't raise his observation with either Leigh or me.'

5

I t was nice to feel safe, knowing I was ensconced in what I guessed was four-and-a-half-star accommodation: fitting given the sort of day we'd just been through. The only off-putting thing was the lack of windows and that the only door to the outside world was locked ... from the outside.

'You'll get used to it soon enough Les,' Clam genially tried to reassure me. Fancy a cold beer?

'Yeah, that'd be good. But tell me, where's my Nissan?'

'Ahh, now that's a reasonable question, but I'm afraid I honestly have no idea, and if I did I couldn't tell you anyway. However, I can assure you it's in good hands and receiving a lot of mechanical tender loving care. I hope you'll like its new colour, and classy newfangled NSW rego plates.'

'Bloody Hell Clam, what's next? They gunna paint me black to match you perhaps, or what?'

'Hadn't thought of that. They could of course, but you're more likely to get fitted with a hairpiece to match mine.'

'But you're damn nearly bald!'

'That's right, but you can't have hair and expect to have brains. I'm sure our boys could arrange for you to have a moustache instead; that could really suit yah mate.'

I was rapidly becoming aware of this bloke's sense of humour and of his pragmatic view on life, but it was his self-confidence and demonstrated survival skills which impressed me most.

* * *

TOGETHER WE PREPARED AN EXCELLENT SALAD, cooked chips in the air-fryer and grilled rib-eye fillet steaks to medium rare. Clam searched the refrigerator and found a tub of salted caramel ice cream, a flavour I'd not previously tasted. It was fab so I helped myself to a second serve.

I then searched the pantry and found some pre-ground, 100% Australian grown arabica coffee and a bottle of coconut flavoured syrup.

A brew was soon on the make and about six minutes later I filled two mugs: strong and black, no milk.

As Clam was about to take his first sip, I surprised him somewhat as I quickly added a slug of the coconut syrup to his mug.

'I hope you're not trying to poison this fine blackfella; what's that muck anyway?'

'It won't kill you; go on, try it.' He did, albeit tentatively at first.

'Ehhmmm; mate, that's bloody good, eh? I'll be having seconds of that.'

* * *

AFTER OUR MEAL we watched the ABC news and then Sky News for an hour or so. There being nothing of interest we cleared away the aftermath of our dinner, turned off the TV and settled into large, adjustable lounge chairs.

'Now would be as good a time as any to have a proper chat wouldn't you say Clam?'

'Agreed. And I can guarantee there will be no interruptions this time.'

We relaxed in each other's company and talked frankly, until late into the night.

* * *

FOR OPENERS, Clam said, 'I owe it to you Les, to provide you with a bit about my background and why it is that my boss picked me to find you, and to deliver you here, unharmed, like.'

'That'd be a good start,' I replied calmly, 'and I acknowledge how you've done that, but I must say the blasé way you killed that bloke at Dinner Plane was unnerving.'

'That's in part due to my formal training Les, and part by our need to even up the odds against a bloody dangerous enemy. The balance of my behaviours was dictated by my ancestral genes which still come in handy from time to time. But let's not dwell on that, eh.'

'But still, this's serious stuff Clam. I need to get my head around why I'm so damn important to you blokes.'

'I won't give you the full-blown account,' Clam replied firmly, 'I have no authority to do that, but I can give you the broad-brush story.

'In the meantime, you'll just have to accept that my job is to keep you alive while our boys in the field explore your background. You must also understand mate, that should anyone implicate me with your protection, or otherwise, I'll deny everything. Regardless, we both must remain very careful not to leak anything to anyone, particularly news media reporters.'

'Still, I feel uneasy about how all of this has erupted so quickly.'

'OK Les, that's understandable; we're talking grand larceny ... unrecovered multiple and huge thefts of personal property, with international security implications probably involving multiple murders.

'So, Les, have you ever dabbled in diamonds?'

'Well, yes, as a matter of fact I did once, albeit it'd have to have been more than thirty years ago. Did a favour for a bloke,' I replied lamely. 'Low risk stuff and it paid well; I never entertained having another crack at smuggling. Besides he'd probably be dead by now.'

'What kind of a favour was that, Les? ... and what makes you think he's dead?'

'I think he's dead because I heard a rumour on the black-market grapevine: it was a reasonably reliable source of info back in those days. But if you're asking me if I witnessed his dead body, then no I didn't ... and besides I've never heard his name mentioned since.

'I acted alone, as a basic courier; just one small package of uncut diamonds delivered to an Antwerp address. But, as I said, that was about thirty years ago and I swear I've never done anything like that again.'

'Perchance Les, would that bloke have been known as The Diamond Whisperer?'

'Jesus H Christ,' I blurted; arms out wide, aggressively demanding, 'how could you possibly know that Clam?'

'Chill Les. You should realise by now that our operatives are dedicated folk who move in mysterious ways. We have it on good advice that that chap's name was recently intercepted, and it carried a strong message that an Australian arsehole, that's you Les Harper, have a significant price on your head.'

'For *what*, precisely?'

'Betrayal apparently. It seems you failed to perform a simple delivery job, the outcome of which meant that you were, back then, and still are today, the only person alive who knows his identity ... and big money is out there to eliminate you.'

'Ahh, c'mon Clam, that's gotta be total bullshit! I made that delivery as agreed and got paid for it. I had no reason to betray him.'

'I believe you Les, but we must assume two things. First, he thinks otherwise and is hopefully confusing you with someone else, and second, that our man is not dead, is back in business and doesn't want anyone other than himself to survive a major heist he has in mind.'

'Well Clam, your intel must be much better than mine. I can't argue that, but truly, I haven't thought about what I was doing thirty or more years ago, of late, so I must accept what you're telling me I suppose.'

'I think you've got the message now mate. I trust you, and I hope and expect you to trust me.

'Think about it Les, in a day or two you'll be an entirely different bloke with a serious role to play in arresting some nasty operator, or operators, so it's best that we're all on the same page.

'Like I hinted at earlier, you're in for a hell of a makeover; new hair style and colour, altered dental work, eye shape alteration, a wardrobe of a new style of clothing and footwear; posher like, I suspect. And from that time, not even your mother will recognise you.

'And oh yes, every document which could have previously identified you is no doubt in the process of being deleted or removed from existing records.

'You'll also get a new name and Australian passport, a different driver's license, an ANZ bank account with regular monthly deposits … and of course, an as new, 4 litre, AWD Pathfinder.'

'Do I get a gun to go with that?'

'Most likely, yes, but we'll decide that after you've excelled and completed a bit of special training.'

'Excelled!? I'm too bloody old for this sort of caper.'

'Maybe so Les, but you do want to stay alive until after we complete this little project? Yes? Like me, mate, whether we like it or not, we are both now disposable commodities.'

'Oh Christ, just what I wanted to hear. And when pray tell does all this kick off?'

'As soon as your new self is available and we've sorted safe accommodation for you.

'But that's enough on that for now, let's have another beer and get to know a bit more about each other. I'll start if you like?'

6

***

Leaning back into my chair, I tried forcing myself to relax; instead, the effects of the beer were taking over nicely. I sighed, deeply, then casually waved an arm in Clam's direction. 'OK young fella, you may now proceed.'

'Right kind sir, I shall. I'll first disclose things in a nutshell like, but then if you want me to elaborate, I will, but there will always be things about me which I can't divulge.'

'Understood, I don't want you to justify your being my bodyguard, but I do want to better understand where we're headed with all this.'

'OK. Well, I started my working life after completing a Bachelor of Arts degree at Melbourne Uni, in Social and Political Sciences, specialising in anthropology and criminology. I may have been the first black fella to do that, and to achieve honours.

'Nevertheless, I was encouraged by one of my tutors to apply for a scholarship to attend the Duntroon Military Academy here in Canberra. I won that scholarship, met some really switched on white fella's who became work colleagues and lifelong friends.

'After graduation, four of us were head hunted by the Australian Federal Police to work as field operatives investigating and arresting those who were intent upon making an ill-gotten fortune reselling stolen livestock, not to mention invading homesteads to obtain money and relieving farmers of any valuable goods they could get their hands on. A lot of those thieves were murderous bastards and had no regard for the impact their actions had upon farmers and their families. Several honest, hard-working farmers took their own lives: those that didn't still had little or no police support.'

At this point, Clam rose from his armchair, walked to the fridge and relieved it of another two cans of beer. Without ceremony, he handed me one and opened his with a flourish.

'It's a remarkable thing Les,' he said as he walked back to his chair, 'that so much rural theft has gone on for so long, and unpunished. It still is unfortunately but given another decade we might be rid of that scourge.

'Eventually those in power here in Canberra got the message. It was agreed that an elite Livestock Theft and Home Invasion Task Force would be established, financed and trialled for two years; one team of five special police officers for each state. Two of my Duntroon mates and I were seconded to form the Victorian team.'

Clam paused, took a hearty swig from his can, belched loudly then continued.

'We had several rewarding wins with cooperation from local police; those like us from the other states and from farmers of course. All our operations, though prioritised and sanctioned by Canberra, were planned, overseen and led by a retired drover. His name will never appear in any records, but he had a wealth of knowledge about managing properties and stock, organisation and inspiring people. Bloody courageous old bugger too, and he had a real knack with handling dogs ... one, which I'll tell you about one day.

'Anyway, in my second year of service I was assigned to track the movements of a particularly nasty Vietnamese bloke, who as it was later revealed, had murdered thirteen farmers.

'I eventually nailed him, but his legacy remained. Not only had he set up a network of blokes to carry out many other thieving operations, but he and his wife were harbouring a German bank note counterfeiter.'

Before Clam could continue, I interrupted. 'By *nailing*, I assume you mean *killing*?'

'Yep; he was armed, had already fired at me twice, and just missed … but I was faster and a better shot than him. Let's leave that for now, eh?

'We also uncovered another side venture which had interested that Vietnamese couple: dealing in stolen fine art. By that I mean actually doing the stealing, storing and reselling valuable paintings at auctions in Europe.

'Yet despite all these revelations, there was always the inkling someone else was orchestrating everything dodgy going on in rural Australia, but from afar.

'Anyway, our success resulted in me being seconded to work with the Belgian Police on an ongoing operation designed to put an end to that smuggling racket. We did it, the only casualty was me: I got shot in the arse!'

My laughter was immediate but didn't seem to offend Clam. 'Obviously you survived mate, so I assume you were pensioned off and returned to Australia?'

'Oh no. Getting shot was one of the best things to ever happened to me,' Clam replied, though his face displayed no pleasure at his recollections. 'If that hadn't happened, I would never have met my beautiful, wonderful wife.'

An awkward pause followed. 'There's more you want to tell me mate?'

'Yes, but I'll take no joy in the telling.

'She nursed me back to health and somehow, in the hospital where she worked, we fell in love. Me a black fella from Oz and her, the most beautiful Belgian woman you could ever lay your eyes on.

'You can imagine my surprise when shortly after I was released from hospital that I learnt her true employer was the Belgian Secret Service, who had assigned her to look after me so that I could join her team in Europe to dismantle a diamond smuggling cartel and arrest the principal perpetrator.'

Another awkward pause followed, but this time my attention was drawn to the tears now rolling down Clam's cheeks.

I moved to get up from my chair intending to provide comfort to my friend, but he raised his hand and said, 'Don't get up Les, let me finish ... you need to know the rest.'

That pause continued for a few more seconds before Clam said while trying to stifle a sob. 'The bastard showed no mercy; he killed my wife with one shot to her temple.'

At last, the penny dropped. Clam was after revenge! Which means he probably knows more about our intended target than I do. To give Clam pause to compose himself I got up and started to make a pot of coffee. 'Milk and two sugars with a dash of coconut essence. Right?'

Clam nodded.

The coffee having steeped long enough, and several minutes having lapsed without any further conversation, I said to Clam as I handed him his brew, 'Mate, I've got a few questions, is that OK?'

'Yep, go for it.'

'Just two questions for now; is Clam your real name and why is our apparent target called The Diamond whisperer?'

'Actually, my real name is Callum. The name *Clam* came about when I was a young kid. Apparently it was easier for my little friends to say Clam, than Callum ... so, *Clam* it's been ever since. However, my surname is of no consequence; in civilised society I don't exist. Even my mob's name is too vague to be understood and therefore of no use to anyone. So mate, don't ask.

'As for The Diamond Whisperer, well that nickname surfaced through the diamond trade via the cartels, who for generations have operated outside the legal diamond trading business.

'Our man operates solo in opposition to those cartels and probably has many loyal contacts across the world. Obviously he exists, but nobody has any idea how, or where he headquarters himself.

'Small smash and grab thefts from jewellery shops are not usually his mode of operating unless he gets a whiff about it beforehand. The *would-be* perpetrators apparently receive *a not to be misunderstood threat* that their intended job will be exposed to the police unless they cough up a sizeable cash payment in advance. Blackmail, of course.

'Few fail to comply, and those who don't, either sensibly cancel their plans, or proceed, but even if they succeed, are soon relieved of their entire haul ... to be fenced by the Whisperer when it best suits him. We think that's him just playing games, and a cute way of maintaining a safe, regular access to easy cash.

'However, his penchant is that he seems to have the ability to make diamonds disappear without a trace at the first hint of a major package being transferred between the world's recognised legal trading houses. And worse, those disappearances have often been accompanied by the murder of low-level cartel operatives, secret services officers and innocent people ... including my wonderful and brave wife. Which, of course, makes it extremely difficult for people like us to gather evidence regarding his identity, or where he is at any time.

'So Les, perhaps you can now see why *you* are so important to us; you just might be able to recognise him ... without him having any idea he's being set up.'

* * *

MIDNIGHT WAS APPROACHING, but Clam hadn't quite finished. 'Here Les, read this,' he said as he retrieved a folded piece of paper from his wallet and then handed it to me. It read: -

On March 3, 1942, a Dutch Dakota DC-3, PK-AFV, carrying an extremely valuable package of diamonds from Amsterdam was shot down by a Japanese Zero fighter plane over Western Australia. Those diamonds were intended for safekeeping in Australia during the Nazi invasion of Europe. The plane, dubbed the "Diamond Dakota," was forced to crash-land on a beach at Carnot Bay, near Broome. Four people died in the crash, and a number were injured, but the survivors were rescued by locals from Beagle Bay. The fate of the diamonds, valued at many millions of dollars today, remains a mystery, with some claiming that Jack Palmer, a beachcomber, found and kept some of them.

Another jolt of realisation struck. I read that article again then handed the slip of paper back to Clam.

'That's the earliest official record of account, but there's more I can tell you,' Clam said while trying to suppress a yawn, 'but mate, that'll have to wait until tomorrow, because I'm goin' tah bed.'

As you can imagine I didn't sleep all that well that night. Memories I thought forgotten tormented me, yet I did get to sleep when I eventually surrendered to the blurring influence of downing five cans of full-strength beer.

7

At some ungodly hour, I was gradually roused by someone gently nudging me on my shoulder. Low level artificial light, the majestic refrains of Antonin's Dvorak's New World Symphony, plus the exquisite aroma of freshly brewed coffee permeated my bedroom: all definitely not what I was expecting. The anticipated hang-over was non-existent, adding a further unexpected delight to this new day.

'Here Les, get this into yah before the sun burns yah bloody eyes out. Then rise and shine, yah can't stay in bed all day; besides I've already done a day's work.'

'OK. OK. I don't need to be told twice mate, but first I need to pee, so stand aside or lose a limb!'

* * *

BREAKFAST WAS MINIMALIST. Orange juice, a couple of slices of toast with plum jam and a second cup of coffee. Unexpectedly, about ten minutes later the front door to our safe house opened and in walked Leigh.

'Good morning boys,' our young bodyguard called out brightly.

He was wearing a black tracksuit, runners and beanie. 'Here, you'll need these, matching training gear. Put these on if you would please, and quick like. We need to get a move on while it's still dark. Can't have anyone paying us too much attention, eh?'

'Fresh air and training mean exercise,' I replied unenthusiastically and adding, 'not what I was expecting either.'

'Ah, come on, don't be like that Les, this is the best time of day.'

Surprisingly, I thoroughly enjoyed the outing walking briskly between Clam and Leigh, returning to our house just as the sun was casting its first shards of sunshine through a cold and typical foggy Canberra morning.

'Well done, Les,' said Leigh. 'You've just completed your maiden early morning walk while you're in our care. You do realise that you've just done four k's without a rest? We'll have you jogging in no time.

'Anyway, I'll leave you to it,' Leigh added as he opened the front door for us. 'I'm meeting Thommo in a few minutes for a gym work-out. Oh, and don't be shocked to find that your beds have been made and everything has been cleared away. Catch yah both later.'

Leigh purposefully closed the front door behind him with a solid clunk: a noisy double click followed as his key locked that only door.

* * *

Having showered and freshened up, I dressed in the casual clothes laid out upon my bed; a nice choice I must say but having one's own butler (whoever that person was) was another first for me

'I say Clam, you were about to elaborate on that Diamond Dakota which the Japs shot down.'

'Correct. I'll get started, then it's over to you.'

'Though the Dakota's engines were damaged, the pilot, Ivan Smirnov, was also injured and some passengers were killed, either during the Jap attack or in the crash landing. Yet Ivan had somehow managed to land the plane without totally destroying it.

'A rescue team removed those who had died, and they helped the survivors to reach safety. That rescue was led by Warrant Officer Frederick "Gus" Clinch. He's no longer a person of interest but interestingly the package of diamonds was lost during the crash. The subsequent fate of that package remains a mystery, but Les, our team's speculation is the reason we are still working on this case.

'Interestingly, another local bloke, a beach scavenger called Jack Palmer, allegedly found that missing package, and supposedly helped himself, keeping some of the package's contents; hence he earned the nickname, Diamond Jack.

'Clearly during that chaotic crash and its aftermath, many have since speculated about the opportunity that could have been created. Lives had been lost, and people were injured and in great peril of dying, so few, if anyone, would have known about the diamond package.

'It remains rumour that some of the diamonds were recovered and supposedly returned to the authorities, though that has not been proven.

'Palmer had associates who were all rounded up, their dwellings and properties thoroughly searched then all were charged with theft. All were acquitted based on the lack of evidence.

'Some diamonds *were* subsequently recovered, as I said, though very little is known about their current location. Which means the whereabouts of the balance of that fortune is still unknown.

'You might also be interested to know that within six months or so of their trial, all of Palmer's associates had disappeared ... until local aboriginals found their bodies.

'According to local knowledge, Palmer had also disappeared; not a word to anyone, and no forwarding address was left at the Broome post office.

'Which meant, we thought, that Palmer found that diamond package, and if he's still alive, has them squirreled away in a safe place. He may also have off-loaded some of those diamonds to the local aboriginals to ensure they would get him well away from Broome ... though what they would have done with those stones is anyone's guess.'

'And assuming he's still alive, he must be early ninety something,' I added.

'Most likely, yes, he would,' Clam replied, nodding his confirmation of my layman's analysis. 'But you'd be wrong to assume Diamond Jack was ever our prime suspect; he's also been long dead, and no diamonds were found either on or near his body; another victim of a single shot to the head.'

'And yet someone *still wants me dead*! And it's now also my guess that a trip to Broome is on the cards to give you a chance to question some the local aboriginal elders to see what you might dig up; no pun intended.'

'Right again Les,' Clam said admiringly, 'you're getting bloody good at this stuff, and as soon as your make-over's finished, that's exactly where we're going.

'We won't be alone though, Leigh and Thommo will have arrived a week or so beforehand to do some reconnoitring. They're the best at that caper and will unearth any undertow of antagonism or suspicious activities which could upset our own information gathering agenda.'

I should have bit my tongue but blurted out, 'I know this'll sound a bit picky Clam, but I hope they both have dirt under their fingernails if they intend to be accepted as cattlemen for example, like.'

Clam looked at me in a manner I'd not seen before; suddenly unfriendly, lips tight pressed, eyes asquint and brow wrinkled. 'Don't get too smart-arsed, Les. Those men are putting their lives on the line for you. They were embarrassed by you having so easily exposing what could have been a life-or-death oversight. But don't worry, that detail has and will be addressed.'

* * *

WE TOOK A BREAK, silently agreeing to leave that awkward moment at arm's length, and to move on.

It was finally time to spill my guts, yet I had another question. 'I should have asked you this earlier Clam, but before my make-over starts, is it legal what you blokes are planning for me? I haven't signed anything which formally gives my consent.'

'It's now too late to be worrying about that mate; Les Harper as you were previously known, no longer exists.'

Yet, I pondered; hopefully Clam's earlier advice that *I could become expendable*, meant in name only.

There it was again, another jolt of reality confirming I was powerless to opt out; yet truthfully, my curiosity was in overdrive.

8

———————

I put aside the remnants of my coffee, relaxed back into the comfort of my armchair and launched into what I hoped would be a helpful chronology of my adult life.

'In forty-two, at the time that Dakota was shot down, I was eighteen and had been posted to the Middle East immediately after I'd completed my National Service Training in Queensland.

'*En-route* to the Middle East, my brigade of fresh reinforcements was redirected to New Guinea to help delay the Japs from advancing southward.

'Soon after, for reasons best known only to the Poms at that time, Australia agreed to re-deploy me and a few of my mates who had all been trained in heavy artillery operation, back to our original destination.'

'That much we already know, Les,' Clam interrupted quietly, though purposefully, 'and we know you served our country with distinction at Tobruk. The problem is, after that, well, we sort of lost track of you.

'I guess that's understandable given all the immediate post-war confusion. Army records were either scarce, or incomplete, or lost; a damn shame that, on many levels. Anyway, mate, enlighten me: in a nutshell, what happened to you after you were demobbed from the Australian Army?'

As if sensing I needed sustenance to fortify me for what I was about to further volunteer, Clam suddenly sprung from his armchair and dashed to the kitchen. After clattering about for five minutes or so, he returned carrying a large serving tray which held not only two mugs of steaming hot coffee, but two huge slices of cream-filled sponge cake, topped with a generous layer of dark chocolate: cake which had mysteriously found its way into our fridge.

Of course, a second serve of that cake followed: a third would have been too much ... and downright ungentlemanly.

I pressed on. 'I chose to join a few of my mates who were determined to visit England. Despite the ruination of vast areas of London by German bombers and those dreadful V2 rockets, we found accommodation on adjoining farms about fifteen miles out of London. Our board and lodgings payment was agreed to be our free labour, doing whatever the farming families needed.

'Money, or rather the depressing lack of it, was a constant annoyance, but by chance I met Ronnie Burgess, a Pommie army sergeant who, unlike me, always seemed to have an abundance of cash ... which certainly was not his army retirement pension.'

'Let me guess Les,' Clam interrupted, 'he was operating illegally in the black-market.'

'Correct. Ronnie and I got on well and I soon started working for him. I knew it was risky work, but he taught me how to play it safe and stay out of jail. It was amazing how much money was still circulating, and it only took me eighteen months before I'd put together a healthy stash.

'It was about then that Ronnie said it was time to do my own thing because he wanted to move to New Guinea and set up a co-existing sugar plantation and rubber extraction operation.

'That gave me the opportunity to return to Australia, but I chose not too; Ronnie would need help. We agreed upon a 50/50 partnership, and we threw ourselves into building an imagined fortune.

'Planting periods were staggered, and local labour took the hard work out of it for us. These workers were loyal, generally with a happy disposition and well paid.

'I thoroughly enjoyed the lifestyle; however, I had two fears ... catching malaria and running out of money. In hindsight, I was very lucky indeed to avoid the former, however, the latter eventually started producing suitable quantities for what turned out to be insatiable markets. Money issues faded quickly, and life was rosy and comfortable.

'We persevered for another eighteen months or so, but world events were changing rapidly again: communist forces had designs on annexing the entire Korean Peninsula. That didn't sit well with the Americans and British and before long a full-blown war erupted in Korea, and of course, Australia followed suit.

'To my great surprise, rather than keeping a low profile and concentrating upon our business operations, Ronnie showed an unhealthy interest in that growing war and bugger me, it wasn't long before he announced he'd had enough of plantation work and intended to immediately join that conflict ... where he assured me, he'd be able to make ten times more money in a year than he ever would being an exporter of sugar and rubber.'

'And let me guess Les,' Clam interrupted, 'I'll bet the black-market was the attraction again. So go on, how'd you receive that news?'

'Correct again. Apparently, his old army mates were already onto this caper, and they were keen to have him back on board. We talked about things at length, but he wouldn't budge from his decision. I had no intention of trying to run our business alone, so we agreed to place our business into a caretaker mode. As luck would have it, Ronnie knew just the right blokes to do this, a retired South African mercenary turned farmer and his two sons. But that's another story.

'Anyway, a deal was done; their time and effort, to be paid from ongoing product profits. No paperwork, just a handshake between mates.'

'So Les, what did you do then?'

'Well I'm not entirely sure why, but I chose to tag along with

Ronnie, after all, I too had accumulated reasonable skills in running contraband operations in a war zone, and if the money that was already being made was any indication and reliable, I stood the chance of being able to retire a very wealthy boy. If that didn't work out, I could always return to plantation life in New Guinea.

'When hostilities ceased, we headquartered in Seoul. This was where and when the big money was up for grabs, for commodities of all description were in high demand. We worked our butts off and accumulated immorally indecent fortunes even by Ronnie's assessment. Though all good things come to an end, it still took the authorities and Americans eighteen months to put sufficient pressure on our operations for us to call it quits.

'Mate, that's enough for the time being, how about lunch?'

'Bloody hell Les, you must be psychic. Our lads should be here in about five minutes. You won't be disappointed in what they offer up. No grog though.'

9

Clam wasn't joking. I don't think I've ever had roast pork cooked so magnificently: tender, thick cuts artfully spiced and with just the right amount of crackling and apple sauce. The five accompanying vegetables were also perfection and equally delicious.

* * *

BACK IN OUR armchairs and nursing our favourite coconut flavoured coffees, I pressed on.

'Did I mention that we squirrelled away our money into Swiss bank accounts for safekeeping? No? Well, we did that fearing it might be destroyed and lost if we lodged our fortunes with English banks which would definitely be the target of German bombing raids.

'Anyway, after visiting post war Europe, and witnessing the carnage inflicted upon England's cities and infrastructure, somehow, Ronnie, bless his adventurous soul, found us—in his estimation—"a risk free, real easy earner" as a courier transferring gems between Bruges and Amsterdam.

'My first transfer was successful, without incident and as

promised, I was paid handsomely in advance by "our employer" …
who I met only once, and albeit for no more than a minute.

'Sadly, that was the last I ever saw of Ronnie. I have no proof what
became of him, but instinctively I knew his number must have been
up, though I had no idea for what reason. Ronnie had been a good
mate, and had taught me many things, but I wasn't going to hang
around and mourn his mysterious demise, deciding that that same
fate would probably be awaiting me.

'Within two days I was back in London preparing for a safe,
relaxing cruise back to Australia. However, about three weeks later,
and with still at least four weeks before my advised departure date, a
most unexpected note and a small locker key were slipped under the
door of my hotel room. It read something like: *You've got something of
mine and I want them back. Using this key, leave my property in locker 721
at the Paddington Station within 24 hours and DO NOT alert the police.
Throw the key onto any of the train lines. Failure to comply will be
extremely painful. TDW.*

'Not wanting to rock the boat so to speak, I made it quick smart to
my nearest bank, relieved my account of three thousand pounds—a
pittance really— and placed that money inside the railway station
locker. Having locked the box, I walked away and discarded the key as
demanded.

'Confident that my *donation* would cover whatever indiscretion I
was supposed to have committed, I exited the station and made my
way to the shipping line office where I'd two weeks previously
booked my passage to Australia. I threw some bribe money around
and got what I wanted: a single room on a ship set to sail in the next
two days.'

'But you couldn't recall that event when I asked you earlier?'
Clam asked with raised eyebrows.

'That all happened a bloody long time ago Clam, but no, subsequently I never thought much about it; I'd done all that was necessary to ensure my safety, and in the years that followed I was
genuinely consumed by other things in a new life.

'To be honest though mate, when you initially asked me about that, few details resurfaced in my brain at that time; those that did were insignificant, or so I reckoned then, to be of much use to you. In hindsight, knowing now what info you've been after, I should have said something earlier. I therefore hope that what I've just been talking about is accepted as the truth.'

'No harm done Les, I don't believe you've been bullshitting, so press on mate.'

'Right, where was I?'

'On a ship bound for Australia.'

'Oh yeah. As soon as we docked in Fremantle my priorities were to find accommodation, and to set in train the transfer of all my English and other mainland European bank deposits into a local branch of the Commonwealth Bank of Australia.

'I didn't expect the latter task would produce immediate results, but within only eight weeks, everything was safely accounted for.

'With regard to accommodation however, because I had no Australian money, I needed a job, and quick like.

'Not only was getting a job a fluke, but that success became another turning point in my life.'

'How so Les?'

'On my first day in Freo, I applied for a labouring job with a local building contractor. The bloke who hired me, Bill Sutton, was tough but genuine, offering me rent free digs if I agreed to stay on for at least two months. He even gave me a fifty quid cash advance until I received my first week's pay.'

'Well, go on Les, there's more, I can tell by that stupid grin on yah face.'

'Yep, there is. I also got to meet Linda, Bill's amazing sister.'

'OK. Stop there Les, you've earned a beer or two. Besides, it's gotta be five o'clock somewhere.'

* * *

About half an hour later, refreshed and suitably relaxed, I settled into my armchair intending to complete the outline of my life story.

However, I'd no sooner opened my mouth than the front door opened and unannounced, in walked Leigh carrying a small bundle. 'G'day boys, don't get up' he chirped happily. 'I've got some good news Les; our med team and I will be here to collect you at four o'clock this arvo to commence your make-over.

'My orders are to tell you to be ready and on time; shit, shaved and showered; OK? Here, Les, you'll also need to be wearing this, it's just normal hospital garb.

'Oh yeah one more thing Les. Stay off the grog and don't drink or eat anything after I leave. Clam will ensure you comply.'

That said Leigh headed for the door, calling out, 'See you at four, eh?'

Another reality moment struck. The consequences of Leigh's abrupt orders and his brisk exit left me feeling slightly nauseous and with trembling hands.

10

———

Clam did his best to distract me, his solution simple.

'Mate, I'll not drink or eat anything either, so let's press on. You were about to tell me about your Boss's daughter.'

'Yes, I was. Well, it became obvious after only a couple of weeks that Linda and I were highly compatible, so high that we married a month later. I gave Bill two months' notice, or whatever time it would take him to find my replacement.

'However, two months later we were in Melbourne.

'Linda had no difficulty finding a job: she was, as it transpired, a trained teacher. I too found a job; no, that's wrong, I found two jobs. In the mornings, before the school day officially started, I drove a refrigerated truck delivering fresh milk to the schools in our area. That was fun; as often as not, the early boys took great pride in helping me offload the milk crates. They didn't have to be told twice that it was OK to call me Les. I guess that made them feel all grown up like. They never learnt my surname, but we were all good *first name mates* and I can't recall if I ever had to discipline any one of them.

'The second job I enjoyed most, though at times it was a bit inconvenient. Because I owned a car, I put myself at the disposal of the local hospital if they needed immediate patient transport following a vehicle accident, or if a woman needed hospital assistance to deliver her baby. I soon learnt that accidents and babies are alike; they wait for nobody!'

'Neither of us had kids and we were both on the wrong side of fifty to have our own. But life was never dull, and we spent nigh on twenty fabulous years together visiting New Zealand, England, South Africa, Peru and Iceland. I could talk to you about that time 'til the cows come home, but we don't have the time, right?'

'Yep, you'd better get a move on mate,' Clam said patiently. 'Just concentrate on the more major events.'

'OK. There's only one event that means anything else to me: Linda died in my arms from a heart attack. God only knows why; she was much fitter than me, never smoked, ate only the best and freshest food and hardly ever drank alcohol. It should've been me who carked it first.

'Losing Linda shattered me, but I soldiered on, drinking far too much and too often. I sold my Melbourne property and moved to Sale, In Gippsland where I lived alone and somehow qualified to receive an age pension, not that I needed it. It was during this time that I got the urge to spend some time in the high country and experience life living above the snow line. And that Clam, is where you found me.'

'Yes, well, that's almost right Les,' Clam said while smiling broadly and theatrically clapping his hands. 'Actually, it was not long before then that we eventually got a lead on your whereabouts. It was a bit of a fluke discovery by one of our researchers who was looking in an archived copy of a Western Australian newspaper for something totally unrelated, and your name bobbed up in the Marriage Notices section. Not a bad effort, given how junior that bloke is, and for how long you'd been on our persons of interest list.

'Our man, no hang on, it was a woman, noted the newspaper's date, guessed at your age, did a name check with the Victorian Bureau of Births, Deaths and Marriages, cross checked with the

Australian Pensioner's Department and bingo, there you were ... and living in Sale; almost right under our noses.'

'Despite what you've been putting me through, that was in the nick of bloody time for sure; remind me to thank her.'

'No need mate, you can do that yourself. She works just down the road and will arrive here with Thommo before you get whisked away for your make-over.'

* * *

I HAD JUST SLIPPED on my medical gown when the front door opened. In walked Thommo and a woman, not the young, well groomed, fresh faced and athletic girl I was expecting, but a mature, bespectacled woman. She was dressed for comfort in jeans and a puffer jacket, her hair long and blond (or was it white?) and hanging down to her shoulders. She was quite attractive despite her apparent age which I guessed was mid-sixties. In a confident, relaxed manner, she spoke first, 'Well g'day Mr Harper, we meet at last. My name's Joan, Joan Davies, but like you I don't have recourse to my birth name.'

We shook hands, her grip firm, her hand warm. 'Great to meet you Joan; if it hadn't been for your eagle eye, I'd be well and truly dead by now.'

'My pleasure Les, but that's been my job for the past twenty years. I've been briefed about you, and I'm sure all will go well with your make-over. And I'm equally sure you'll be in great shape to handle all that follows.'

Before I could reply, Joan said with a mysterious smile. 'Would you believe that I'm only thirty-eight? No? No, I'm not that young, but if the circumstances demanded it, I could still pass for someone that age. Anyway, you're now in the hands of some amazing people.

'Let's grab a seat and have a yarn before the others arrive.

'But beforehand, I'm under orders to give you a little jab; some juice to see that you're nice and relaxed before you leave this place. You can have it in your arm or in your bum if you'd prefer.'

I took the arm shot: never felt a thing.

The next twenty minutes flew by, and I thoroughly enjoyed myself; it made me realise how much I missed good female company.

At precisely four pm, Leigh, Thommo and two male stretcher-bearers arrived.

I was quickly and expertly strapped onto the stretcher. Clam and Joan stood by me to give me comfort, or so I thought. In my now dry-mouthed light-headed state, I heard Clam say to me, while chuckling in my ear, 'Just a little adjustment mate; in case you turn up dead somewhere. Can't have that, eh? Nobody'll be able to recognise you from your dental records; there won't be any!'

Most reassuring I thought cynically ... then all went black.

* * *

APPARENTLY, three days passed by without me being aware. Upon waking I felt weird all over, like having been in a bruising Aussie Rules football game and feeling the aftereffects ... lightheaded and marginally nauseous. My mouth felt strange too; beyond numb, confirmation that I'd just undergone some major dental surgery.

As that numbness subsided, it was replaced by a low-level throbbing pain along my jawline. I tentatively ran my tongue over my teeth. Bloody hell, a full set of choppers no less; and no gaps.

My curiosity aroused, I wanted a mirror; immediately like! My pleas—a mix of somewhat frantic arm movements and unrecognisable mumbling—were reluctantly granted. Annoyingly and frustratingly, only my eyes were exposed from beneath a swathe of bandages which otherwise completely covered my head.

'Everything went beautifully Les', said a masked female figure in a voice that I thought I recognised.

'I think I forgot to tell you Les that I was going to be your dental surgeon. Unfortunately, it'll be a few more days before you get to see my handywork and that of the other micro-surgeons who worked on your face and ears.

'I've got to go now Les, but I want you to try and get some sleep. If you need anything, I mean anything, press the button on this gadget,' the voice said calmly as I wrapped my fingers partially around the help call device ... and partially around the fingers handing it to me.

While urgently attempting to mutter something polite, thankful and understandable through my head bandages, without delay I released my partial grip and then made a successful full-on grab for that hand, all of it, hoping it would be Joan's.

'You need to rest Les. Relax, you're quite safe here. There'll be at least two nurses nearby who'll be monitoring your condition 24/7 ... and I'll call by every day to see if you've been a good boy.

'All's good with me Les, we'll talk again in a few days.'

I relaxed; her hand immediately squeezing mine. Without warning, everything again went completely black.

11

'**M**ate, I've got some news,' said Clam enthusiastically, 'assuming you're up to receiving it?'

I nodded my head; it hurt, so I mumbled what I thought would sound like "OK".

'All your vitals are apparently looking good and in three days' time your surgeons have scheduled a group examination of their handywork. Which means Doctor Joan will soon get her hands on you again.'

Hoping Clam could decipher what I wanted to say, and not betray our rather rapid doctor/patient attraction to each other this time I muttered, 'Aww, airgoh mahyt thnot hat obvyus shoorly?'

'Be that as it may,' Clam replied with a quiet chuckle, 'but there's even better news; how about this? Regardless of your make-over results you'll be getting out of bed immediately after the surgeons have finished with you.

'And wait for it, there's more. Leigh and Thommo have developed a fantastic get-fit-quick gym program, just the thing for a bloke your age who must be in Broome in three weeks' time. I hope you don't like swimming because that's the only thing you'll be missing out on.'

More chuckles filled my hospital room, but the collective mirth was lost on me. Had I been able to make myself clear, I'm sure I'd have said, 'Bastards!' Or something equally appropriate.

* * *

THE FOLLOWING three days passed with rising anticipation of my great unveiling: of being "reborn".

I'd just finished morning smoko when in trooped Joan, two of my ever-vigilant nurses, Dale and Philipa, wheeling a table overflowing with medical paraphernalia, then Leigh, Thommo and two other blokes wearing surgical facemasks; whose names I never did learn. Clam had already explained to me the reasons for those anonymous surgeons to remain thus: it was none of my business and I didn't need to know.

Joan was first to speak. 'This won't take long Les, but please take a seat at the kitchen table. As we remove your bandages there will be some minor discomfort, but not for long. However, tell us to stop if at any stage you experience severe pain. OK, let's get started.'

The nurses insisted upon everyone applying a sanitising solution to their hands, whereafter special tight gloves and facial masks were fitted to all medico's and observers.

It only took Joan a minute or two to painlessly remove all my head bandages. There was an initial silence, then followed "ehms and ahhs", head nodding (of approval I hoped) by all three surgeons, and generous clapping by the onlookers.

In turn, each surgeon made close, meticulous examinations of their respective handywork then retreated into the lounge, no doubt to discuss whether or not my make-over had been a professional success.

Ten minutes passed before the surgeons returned to the kitchen. Again, Joan spoke first. 'Here Les, take this mirror and tell us what you think.'

I wasn't exactly terrified, but I was genuinely uneasy about needing to look into that mirror. But, holding my breath, I did.

Clam, I realised, was now standing next to me with one hand on my shoulder. Nevertheless, I flinched when I saw who was staring back at me.

'Meet Richard, Richard Zarkas,' Clam said enthusiastically.

'Good God Almighty!' was the best I could come up with.

'Tell me truthfully, Richard,' Joan asked quickly and rather clinically, 'ignoring the slight swelling, would your mother ever recognize you as her son, if she were alive now of course?'

'No way, nor would my wife ... even if she too was still alive.'

While staring in disbelief at my new face, I had to admit I liked what I saw. Incredibly, overall, I looked at least twenty years younger. Apart from being bald, my eyes now appeared ever so slightly hooded, my ears no longer stood out and my chin had become slightly more chiselled giving my jaw line a certain confident appearance.

The most unexpected feature however was that I now had what looked like a permanent five o'clock shadow.

I tried to smile. That really hurt, but I got the first glimpse of my new teeth.

'Go carefully Richard,' Joan ordered gently, 'you've had a lot of work done on those teeth and it might be another week or so before you can open your mouth without discomfort. You'll not be eating either steak or apples during that time, but you'll soon get used to eating through a straw.

'And while I'm at it, there are a few rules you must follow. For example, *don't* touch your face. Dale and Philipa, or the relieving nurses, will take care of everything should you have a spill. It's also their job to ensure your head is kept covered with a special antiseptic gel, at least for the next three or four days. They'll also manage your medications should your pain increase or if you need help with your bowels.

'I'll be back in two days' time to check you over again Richard,' Joan said matter-of-factly, 'however, I do believe everything is going exceptionally well and you should be up and about in no time.'

'Take that smirk off your face mate,' Clam interrupted with a cruel chuckle, 'you'll soon be in the gym with Leigh and Thommo; that should be fun too.'

* * *

FOUR DAYS LATER, I joined the Australian Federal Police gym using my new name. That initial session was barely enough to raise a sweat, but the lads weren't finished with me and made me walk the two and a half kilometres back to my accommodation.

My meals (though not Clam's) were shrinking, and I was getting totally fed-up eating through a straw. Worse was getting up before daybreak and enduring three gym sessions each day, each of which was just marginally more intensive than its predecessor.

Towards the end of the second week, my workload increased significantly and to top it off, my three friends insisted I try to run all the way home. I did, which I think surprised all of us.

During the third week they had me running to and from the gym; in fact, I was now actually looking forward to each routine, particularly the early morning run. And nearly every morning, Clam would reinforce his belief that this was the best time of the day ... and not just because most of the world's criminals would prefer to be in bed at this hour.

Three and a half weeks later, at the end of the day's gym work, Thommo unexpectedly announced a further change of plan. 'Richard, this will be our last session at the gym; we're leaving for Broome tomorrow. Clam will fill you in on the details. Mate, you've done a good job, and you should be proud of your efforts.'

'Thanks mate, but I couldn't have done this caper without you two.'

As we exited the gym, Leigh had another surprise awaiting me. 'Right, let's now see how good you really are Richard. Last one back to your digs is a dirty dog!'

Clam, Leigh and Thommo took off leaving me stranded; no consideration, no handicapping ... just good-natured laughter as they rapidly opened a sizeable gap.

It would be a lie if I said that I either overtook or passed them, but it did surprise me how good I felt and that those three boyos never ran out of my sight.

Back at our digs, the lads began clapping me; the last twenty metres having been saved for my best sprint over an imaginary finishing line.

Yes, I was puffing heavily and almost exhausted, but not at death's door.

To my surprise (yes, another one), Joan appeared. Smiling broadly, she threw her arms around me and whispered, 'That, my dear Richard was amazing, far beyond anything we expected from you. Go safely on your assignment, I'll miss you.'

Before I could say anything, Joan broke our embrace and walked purposefully to a nearby red Mazda sedan and drove away.

As I entered our accommodation, little did I realise this would be my last stay at this safe house.

'You do realise Richard,' Clam said with unexpected compassion, 'that Joan is quite fond of you, far more than just one of her patients?'

'I'm glad, but do you reckon I'm too old for her?'

'Of course not. Have you looked in the mirror lately?

'Mate, did I tell you that both of my lovely wives were about twenty years younger than me?'

'Yes Clam, you did. I also read it somewhere that's it's a custom for aboriginal men to marry women much younger than themselves.'

'So, we can agree that age is just a number?' Clam responded thoughtfully, 'and that you must love the one you're with?'

A smart man, my friend Clam.

12

____

'Hey Richard?' Clam asked quietly. 'Did you know it's about two and a half times the distance from Broome, to Paris, as it is from Canberra to Broome?'

'Is that right? I bet that's an estimate though. It's probably better to talk in terms of how many days it'll take us to get to Paris from here. But aren't you putting the cart before the horse thinking about that now? We've got that job in Broome to finish first.'

'Correct. I just wanted you to know there may be nothing to be gained from our visit to Broome; any leads would logically be cold by now. Europe may have to be our next stop, much earlier than we first thought.'

'But we *are* still going to proceed with an investigation in Broome, yes?'

'Oh yes, but not in Broome, in the surrounding country,' Clam replied confidently. 'Us black fella's have ways of recording the past. You know, with songs and dances and certain events being retained by our elders to be passed on to our next generations. I might fluke something, so I've volunteered to *go native*, so to speak. Haven't done that for years, but I'll be absent for perhaps a few weeks.

'As I've already told you, Leigh and Thommo will be in Broome making their own enquiries. You'll probably not see them, but if you do, just ignore them, they won't be offended.

'As soon as I return, we'll be out of Broome post-haste. What you do in the meantime is entirely up to you; I'd suggest though that you spend some time sifting through archived library records for any titbits we might have missed. Concentrate on the period after that Dakota crash: names, strange events or people who might not have belonged to the formal investigations. Maybe someone recalled having heard people talking in an unrecognisable language and reported it to the newspaper. Or they just might have recognised it as Russian, or perhaps Polish but that's a bit of a stretch I realise.

'Regardless, make sure you buy a decent hat, one with a wide brim to protect your head and your ears; I've been told that sunburnt ears can be particularly nasty. And while you're at it buy some insect netting for your hat, to keep the flies off your face, like.'

'All of that sounds like a plan, but I still think you'd rather be in Europe. Why's that?'

Clam looked at me with one of his more serious expressions. 'You're a very perceptive white fella my friend, because that's spot on. You would've found out soon enough, but I see no harm in letting you know now that we received some very interesting information from one of our inspectors who visited the chalet next door to the one where you stayed at Dinner Plain.'

'You mean the place where that little girl and her kitten were staying?'

'Correct. And cop this for a coincidence, those chalet guests departed the day after we escaped. Interesting, eh? The situation transpired that those guests left a forwarding address ... in Poland no less.

'That may be a trap, but at least we now have a name and an address we can focus on. You do realise the woman involved was probably not that child's mother, but more likely set up in advance to spy on you and to try and create a means of keeping you in your chalet through a faked friendship with that girl, or maybe, if the opportunity presented itself ... bump you off before those two thugs arrived to do the job.'

'Bloody hell! Just as well you were in the area then, eh?'

'Yes, you could say that, but we too were prepared for an attempt to assassinate you. And let me remind you it was bloody cold waiting outside in that snowstorm for the right moment to interrupt you. Seriously, had I waited another ten minutes I might not have made it to your front door.'

In silence we reflected upon that timing.

Clam broke that silence with another pearl of information. 'Mate, you might also like to think about your new surname.

'"Zarkas" has its origins in Slavic Polish ancestry ... which just might open a new line of enquiry for us.

'By the way, we depart for Broome tomorrow morning. We'll be picked up at five o'clock and driven to the airport where we'll be given our itinerary. Breakfast will be provided along the way. Most likely we won't be sitting together if we've been booked on a commercial flight, but who knows, a military plane just might be heading to Broome, which means we might be rubbing shoulders with a Federal Minister.'

13

———

We were in luck. By the courtesy and generosity of the Australian Defence Force our flight took us direct to Broome, avoiding a lengthy bus trip from Darwin. Though the plane was a noisy beast and only marginally comfortable, the onboard food was excellent.

The views from our windows were amazing; such a vast panorama of changing pastel colours which few people ever get to truly value.

Two other *"civilians"* were on board. Their appearance may have fooled most people, but their demeanour suggested otherwise. Their destination was vague: somewhere in Indonesia as I recall. They also spent quite a bit of time occupying the pilot's cockpit. Clam confidently suggested they were receiving a final assignment briefing; I disagreed, it sounded more as if they were all related, or on their way to a party.

Anyway, as we exited Broome's airport terminal in search of a taxi, our ADF plane was already just getting airborne and bound for God only knows where.

'Did you see our two associates as we walked through the terminal?' Clam asked casually.

'Nah, just those four or five baggage handlers hanging around,' I replied, 'why?'

'Well mate, perhaps next time you'll pay more attention to your surroundings,' Clam cautioned me.

Our second-floor hotel accommodation was basic and pre-paid for a week. It afforded us a decent view of Carnarvon Street, it being the main shopping and eateries area.

At midnight Clam took his leave. Wearing an old, torn and stained shirt and trousers, he set off barefoot into the night, suggesting as he departed that I should lock the door after him.

* * *

BROOME CERTAINLY HAS CHARACTER. An extremely long, active wharf serving the comings and goings of many types and sizes of ships and boats, both local and international ... and an enormous tide which regularly made life uncomfortable for the uninformed or reckless seafarer.

Regardless, it was never difficult to find yourself immersed in conversation with Japanese, Malays, Chinese, Indonesians or Australians, most being in Broome to trade, whether it be for machinery, engine parts, fuel, livestock, seafood, exotic equatorial fruits, cooking oil, rice and of course, beer, cigarettes and black-market drugs. Most of those traders were friendly enough and "happy to give you the best possible bargain in the Territory, despite trying to keep my six kids from starving to death."

Of course, I thoroughly enjoyed playing along with these folk just to test if I still had it when it came to the etiquette of street bargaining. It boosted my ego to see the look on the faces of some traders when they'd clearly been done over.

However, not wanting to attract too much attention to myself I discretely called off my wins and paid full whack. My good grace was rewarded each time, with, for example, "a pick of the largest prawns," or "a phone number if I lookee for naughty." Usually, a handshake and a good laugh was sufficient to ensure we parted company on friendly terms.

Nevertheless, Broome has two downsides, both of which were thrust upon me from day one, that is, it's overbearing humidity and the God-awful, bloodthirsty sandflies!

These irritations made the Broome Museum the most amazing retreat, providing gentle, continuous air movement via a couple of ancient, yet amazingly quiet overhead fans. Double mesh mosquito screens on each ventilation point also worked very effectively to keep the sandflies out.

There were few other tourist attractions, other than a refreshing walk on the jetty, so it was easy to realise why drinking cold beer was almost mandatory. Yet, I felt bored with that pastime and soon needed to do something constructive. So I started sifting through the museum's archives to see what could be gleaned about the aftermath of that famous plane crash in March,1942.

For no specific reason I can remember, I was suddenly struck by a few thoughts that none of us had previously discussed ... as obvious as they probably were at that time.

Logically, nobody on that ill-fated Dokota military plane would have known it was destined to be shot down near to Broome, or why, let alone by a Japanese Zero carrier-based fighter plane. That being the case we were therefore investigating a mass murder since shooting down that plane was surely not an act of war, but rather a matter of theft, occasioning deliberate mass murder.

14

———

At about ten pm on the nominated day for Clam's return to
Broome, I was awakened by him gently punching my
shoulder. That startled me a bit.

'How the hell did you get in, Clam?' I asked groggily, albeit glad to
see that it was him.

'Yes, I'm well, thank you Richard. I'll teach you how it's done one
day. But right now, do me a favour mate and make me a cuppa would
yah while I have a shower and freshen up, like. Make enough for all
four of us; our friends should be here shortly.'

No sooner had Clam returned to the lounge, now dressed in clean
shorts and a t-shirt, than the front door opened again, and in walked
Leigh and Thommo.

'Greetings and salutations lads,' I said jovially, then shook hands
with each of them in turn. Both were in clean clothes and barefoot,
like Clam. 'Grab a seat while I finish pouring the tea.'

Having handed around the mugs of tea, I fetched the last of my
biscuit supply. 'I'm afraid that's all I can offer lads, make the most of
it. I assume you should all have a hearty appetite, come breakfast.'

Clam replied, 'All good by us mate. I for one love them jam filled
one's.'

A minor scramble for those biscuits ensued, however soon after, Clam broke the silence.

'Well so far then, everything seems to be going to plan, so, let's debrief. I'll go first.'

Clam coughed a few times to clear his throat then said, 'My black brothers from two regions I visited were able to recall the incident in question, but not much more than that.

'The third mob, after somewhat of a twitchy start, eventually had a few things to say; apparently, they were called upon to guide three white fellas to the crash site. They could hardly understand a single word: those white fellas spoke in a language they'd never heard before.

'Anyway, they showed me where they reckon that Palmer bloke was killed and buried; not much to see, just a few rocks piled randomly near the base of a cliff. They couldn't tell me whether he'd been shot or pushed from that cliff.

'Many years later, a learned member from a neighbouring mob told them, "that that language was from a place called Poland ... on the other side of the world."

'Unfortunately, though, the old bloke who told that story is long dead, as are most, if not all members of the same mob who went to rescue survivors of that plane crash. That fits with most of what we already know.

'That's almost it; interesting, eh? Interesting that those three initial white blokes got onto the crash site so quickly.'

'So, what did you two unearth?' Clam asked, having turned to face Leigh and Thommo directly, to give them the cue to contribute their findings.

'We can't top that Clam,' Leigh replied. 'But we thought it might be useful to know if any of the local cattle grazier's know the where-abouts of that Dakota.'

'And?' I asked, impatient to know the answer.

'No one knew bugger all,' Thommo replied dejectedly. 'It wasn't that those graziers were hiding anything, they just didn't know, besides there's nothing in it for them to conceal that sort of thing.'

A few yawns were surfacing, but then I asked, 'Does anyone want to know what I've discovered?'

'Can it wait until tomorrow?' Clam suggested with a sigh.

'Probably not mate.'

Regardless, I pressed on; perhaps time was of the essence.

My telling of those thoughts which occurred to me when in the cool confines of the Broome Museum only took a few minutes. However, the alarmed looks on the faces of my three colleagues was special, bordering on being gobsmacked yet professionally appreciating the consequences of my logic.

Leigh was first to speak after I'd finished talking. 'Bravo Richard, you've certainly put the cat amongst the pigeons if your insights prove to be correct. Either way mate, you can't retire until after we complete this investigation. You do know that, eh?'

'I certainly won't contest any of that with you, Leigh,' said Clam thoughtfully. 'Our friend Richard here is probably a step or two ahead of us. So, first thing tomorrow, I'll contact Canberra with our findings; it should be interesting to hear what they have to say. But in the meantime, let's all bloody well get some sleep.'

15

———————

The next morning, Clam mercilessly woke me. I barely had time to prop myself up in the bed than he thrust a mug of sweetened black tea into my hands. 'Here, mate, get that into yah then hit the shower and get dressed. We're leaving in fifteen, no, twelve minutes. The bus driver's assured me he won't wait for anyone.'

We all made it in time to get on board the bus thanks to having packed the night before what luggage we had. There were only five other passengers, a black woman and four kids, presumably all hers.

As the bus moved off, Leigh and Thommo got up from their seats and started moving towards the driver. I noticed that Clam surreptitiously slipped something into Leigh's hand as he walked by.

A brief conversation with the bus driver followed, and yes, I was close enough to eavesdrop.

'Fifty bucks if you can get us to Darwin half an hour earlier than you would normally take,' Leigh asked politely enough.

'That'll be two hundred bucks, total like, for the four of yah,' demanded the bus driver, equally polite.

Thommo leaned in close to the driver's ear and said in a much less polite tone, 'be buggered mate, it'll be seventy bucks all up, and you won't get tossed off this rattle trap.'

'It's a deal then,' replied the now flustered bus driver, 'But I'd suggest you all put your seat belts on.'

* * *

About five miles up the road from Broome, the aboriginal woman started screaming on top note for the driver to stop. 'But it's another twenty miles to where you normally get off, Biddy,' the driver yelled back to her.

'I doan giv no rat's arse, let me orf right now, right 'ere!'

The driver looked at Thommo and shrugged his shoulders seeking approval to stop. Thommo nodded his consent, and the bus shuddered and skidded to a stop, raising clouds of orange dust. Within seconds Biddy was bustling her kids from the bus and couldn't resist a parting jibe at the driver as she climbed down to the ground. 'Wot's got inta yah Sam, yah bloody fool. You on somthin' an wonna kill us all? I'se gunna report yah soon's I get back tah Broome dat's for sure.'

'Sorry Biddy, but one of the other passengers is real crook and needs to see a doctor quick smart like,' Sam (whose name we all now knew) yelled back to her with that devious, blatant lie. To no doubt emphasise the potential validity of that bogus emergency, Sam flattened the accelerator and ripped his other foot from the clutch ... which naturally sent an impressive rooster tail of stones and dust all over Biddy and her kids.

In my mind's eye, I can still today see Biddy giving us an energetic, double handed, two finger salute: though I can only guess at what she was mouthing off at us ... and at what other expletives she was about to add once that cloud of rubble descended fully upon her.

The remaining drive to Darwin can only be described as alarming. Yet Sam made good his word, getting us unscathed to the outskirts of Darwin well before his normal scheduled arrival time.

'Good job Sam,' Thommo said with genuine appreciation, 'but now please get us to the Darwin City Police Station, asap like.'

'No problem's mate, we'll be there in about eight minutes.'

Again, true to his word, Sam stopped the bus at our destination on time, though, simultaneously, so too did a police car directly behind the bus, lights still flashing and siren blaring.

As we descended to ground level, each of us gave Sam a thankful pat on his shoulder. Thommo however, also handed him a hundred dollar note and said, 'keep the change mate, you've earned it. And don't worry about getting a speeding ticket, we'll take care of matters to see that you don't.'

I'm reasonably confident our driver was somewhat bemused to see Clam, a well-dressed aboriginal man, berating the officers in the police car for interrupting our business.

It wasn't long before Leigh gave a thumbs up signal to a now somewhat relieved Sam and then waved him away from the kerb outside the police station. Had Sam hung about he would have witnessed something even more bemusing; that of Leigh and Thommo *courteously escorting* both confused police officers into the Darwin Police Head Office.

We were welcomed by an equally confused duty sergeant, who, to his credit, quickly escorted us to meet the Station's Captain. The Police Captain, David Orr, also to his credit, dismissed his sergeant then suggested that we all be seated.

I watched David's expression with interest. When Clam addressed him and quickly introduced each of us in turn, he leant back into his chair, his eyebrows raised as if slightly alarmed.

Clam continued politely, it now being obvious to David just who was responsible for our unexpected intrusion. 'Here, sir, this document best explains who we represent and why we need your assistance.

'I'm not authorised to provide you with the specifics of our work, but we need your support ... and time is of the essence.'

David leant forward and graciously relieved Clam of his offering. While reading that document David occasionally pursed his lips and drew in his breath to create a slight whistling noise, then punctuating this with a few nods. Having read that document, he composed himself and said, 'I've got no intention of getting into a blue with Canberra, so, Clam, what exactly can I do for you? My station and officers are at your disposal.'

'Thank you, David,' Clam replied politely. 'First, please make sure that Sam, the driver of the bus who dropped us here, does not receive a ticket for speeding, he was, after all, on government duty, you'll agree?

'Second, it seems we may have upset one of my people on our way here; a lovely lady from Broome, named Biddy. She has four kids, and it'd be nice if you could arrange something for her, on our behalf like. You know, such as reimbursing her for not getting the full value for the cost of her interrupted bus fare.'

'Consider both done, but what is it you really need?' David asked with unexpected enthusiasm.

'I need a secure line for a private conversation with my boss in Canberra ... to acquaint him with our situation; and then we'll need some quickish transport to your airport.'

'Right, you can use my office Clam, but first I need to set up your call; it'll only take a few seconds. I guarantee you'll get all the peace and privacy you need in here.

'In the meantime, you lads, why not go outside for a cuppa and introduce yourselves to my officers. I'll join you out there shortly.'

Clam rejoined us ten minutes later and we were whisked away to the airport, sirens *hee-horing* and lights flashing: compliments of Police Captain, David Orr. He then quickly escorted us to the check-in counter where surprise, surprise, the Qantas staff were waiting for us with our tickets and boarding passes, compliments of Canberra.

That entire meeting experience, in fact that entire day, was nothing like what I was expecting. And then, just as David announced he'd have to get back to his office, it was good to shake his hand and to thank him for his hospitality. A good copper, and a decent bloke to boot.

Better, was that I witnessed the makings of a respectful friendship between David and Clam, if their robust handshake was any guide.

16

Despite the urgency associated with our dash to Darwin, our flight was delayed. Annoying in one sense, but in another, it gave us time to discuss what was ahead of us ... and that gave me a timely and fortuitous opportunity to initiate some potentially useful conversation.

'As you can see from our ticketing arrangements our destination is still set for Singapore. However, it seems we'll be having a stopover in Port Moresby to refuel, or offload cargo, and it so happens I'm quite familiar with the forwarding flight from Port Moresby to Singapore. My then business partner Ronnie Burgess and I, used that flight on occasions when we were learning how to become the owners of a successful rubber-tree plantation and to look for sales opportunities once we were fully operational.'

Almost as an afterthought, I added, 'By the way, Singapore has a fascinating history and remains the only Island Nation in the world, yet it still has strong post WW2 ties with England.'

Judging by the looks of anticipation on the faces of my audience urging me to continue, it seemed only natural I should push on. But Leigh quickly interrupted me. 'I didn't know Singapore produced rubber.'

'It does, but only little. The major growers of rubber trees operate in the surrounding countries, like Malaysia to the north and Indonesia to the south. But Singapore remains an important business and export hub; where most of the trading of rubber is conducted, alongside other enterprises not considered entirely legal.

'Anyway, over time we had a few dealings with an Australian entrepreneur who owns a couple of shops in Singapore and has no sense of guilt about selling anything from bedding, clothing, kitchen ware, shoes ... and jewellery, if the price's right.'

'And so, Richard, I do believe we have a potential lead?' Clam added enthusiastically.

I smiled and replied, 'let's hope.'

As if on cue, our loading instructions commenced, but I felt compelled to add another pearl of advice. 'You should all know that on this flight, but more so on the following leg, it can get somewhat bumpy from turbulence, particularly now that the monsoon season's approaching. So, if you need to go to the dunny, go now while you've still got time.'

* * *

BOTH LEGS of our flight were as I'd predicted, though I'd experienced worse. The worst part was the deafening noise from the plane's engines, which not only ruled out conducting any meaningful conversation between us, but made it damn near impossible to sleep.

Our arrival was uneventful and probably witnessed by only a few people. Nevertheless, we immediately now had a new force of nature to cope with: the mid-afternoon temperature, which was in the low thirty degrees centigrade, and the goddam humidity, which was so high, that if any one of us could spit, it was likely to trigger a rainstorm.

Immediately having exited the terminal, we were mobbed by taxi and rickshaw driver's, all intent on "promising us the lowest fare and best transport service in the entirety of Singapore."

Since I'd experienced this manufactured chaos several times, albeit years ago, I gazed beyond that mob and found what I was looking for; two men hanging back, impeccably dressed and proudly leaning against a brilliantly maintained Chevrolet sedan.

'Rule number one, lads,' I reminded my friends. 'Don't get caught up in a conversation with this lot; just follow me, but don't be rough with them, or impolite, we are after all, guests of Singapore. If you have to say anything, just keep saying … already booked, already booked. They'll usually understand that and step aside for you.'

As we broke free from that previously expectant, but now disappointed mob of miscellaneous drivers, Clam said. 'Yah knows what Richard? If I didn't know otherwise, you'd never suspect that Canberra has had a hand in our pickup and transfer.'

'They may well have been,' I replied, but quickly added. 'But I've used this service many times without the slightest hint they might have links with your boss in Canberra, or to anyone else for that matter.'

Twenty minutes later we arrived at the hotel recommended by our drivers. As it transpired, these men were brothers, one the nominated driver, the other being more like a travel advisor who plied us with timely and interesting facts about each region and of the historical significance of various buildings.

"Our" hotel staff were most obliging without being intrusive. Four adjacent third floor rooms were allocated without question and we each received separate keys. Each room was not only cool, but spacious, and comfortably furnished, but also had a private, shaded balcony accessible from the bedroom. And, as we discovered later, this hotel also had a most unexpected phone service, with secured direct lines to Australia's Consulate in Singapore, and to our Canberra contact.

So, Clam won our earlier argument: when he enquired about the cost of our taxi fare and for our accommodation, he was politely advised in clear and concise English. 'That's all taken care of, Sir. We'll only need your signature when you leave us.'

Despite having been sitting, albeit uncomfortably for the past several hours, we agreed to retire to our rooms, freshen up and try to sleep for a couple of hours, then meet back in Clam's room at six thirty.

'I've just been talking with Canberra,' Clam announced as soon as we were all together. 'We've got three days as a stopover here in Singapore before we head for Europe, so we'd best make the best of it we can.'

'For starters,' Leigh said excitedly, 'now that it's starting to cool down, I'm going for a run in that nice looking park over the road.'

'I'll be in that,' Clam immediately agreed.

'What about you Richard?' Thommo asked. 'Are you going to join us?'

'Yeah, why not,' I added with a reasonable degree of enthusiasm. 'But I'll tell you what, if the flying foxes are still roosting, avoid running underneath them.

'May I also suggest that after our run, we have a swim in the hotel's pool and a cold bevvy or two. And then dinner. We won't need to walk very far to find a suitable eatery, and besides, we've got plenty of time on our hands and most people don't start their dinner until after eight o'clock, when the humidity has dropped significantly.

After a sensational "local specialty banquet" and a quiet and reflective stroll back to the hotel in the cool night air, we met back in Clam's room to decide upon a plan of action for the next day or two.

17

After an early breakfast next morning, we sat around the hotel's pool sipping coffee, quietly relaxing and bathing in the sun's first blush of heat.

Suddenly, Clam was on his feet. 'See you back here in ten minutes Richard,' he called over his shoulder and trotted away. 'Shorts, T-shirt and thongs, and don't forget your hat.'

Leigh and Thommo quickly followed suit, not missing Clam's implied order to also get their arses into gear.

'Or your wallets,' I couldn't resist adding as those two lads dashed off to their rooms.

Once we'd reassembled, Clam reiterated our earlier plans. 'Right, we'll be in two teams, Richard and I, and you two. A few things to remember. First, we're playing the stupid Aussie tourist, and second, keep your wits about you regarding being followed. Third, if you purchase anything from any street stalls, don't take offence if the stall handler refuses to shake hands with you; to many people here, their Islamic edicts say that we are worthless infidels, unclean and not to be touched.

'Getting into a blue with them will defeat the purpose of our visit.

We need the local's trust and information, not their hostility, even if we must pay for it. So, keep an eye out for each other's back.

'Otherwise, do whatever you want and see whatever interests you, but be back at the hotel by four thirty. Whichever team arrives back first, is expected to head out immediately to look for the others. I certainly don't want to get the local police involved, far better that you first talk with the hotel manager about the situation.

'As for myself and Richard,' Clam continued. 'It's going to be our objective to locate that Australian ex-pat entrepreneur who Richard mentioned last night.'

'You got any idea where to start looking?' Thommo asked, genuinely interested.

'Of course,' Clam replied with an exaggerated wink and a nod. 'With our understanding and unassuming hotel manager of course.'

* * *

THERE WAS no fuss by the hotel manager to provide us with the address of both jewellery shops, and nor did he probe our intentions. Interestingly, when Clam enquired whether he could also tell us the name of the proprietor, he replied. 'Sir, I do believe you should take that up with your friend here with you,' nodding respectfully in my direction. Yes, I already knew that bloke's name and now knew the addresses of both of his shops, for I'd been given them the previous evening by the hotel manager late the previous evening ... but had forgotten to tell Clam. No big deal.

'I must say, it's becoming rather hot and humid outside,' the hotel manager suggested. 'So, if you gentlemen would prefer to go by taxi, I can have your driver here in two or three minutes.'

'Thank you, we'll accept your suggestion,' said Clam. 'By the way, is it custom to tip the driver?'

'Only if you wish. In your case however, all you need to do is sign the form the driver will present to you. Sign whatever name you wish; I'd suggest not your real name.'

Not only was our taxi driver on time, but he came armed with four bottles of near freezing water which added immensely to the enjoyment of our fifteen-minute road journey.

Clam signed the form presented to us by our driver, thanked him with a twenty USA dollar note for his services, and headed to the first jewellery shop on our agenda.

I was now in familiar territory and not overwhelmed by the volume of foot trade, or the road traffic noise normal for this time of the day. Nor was I surprised by the unrelenting odours and climatic conditions. However, by the disapproving look on Clam's face, I'm sure he would have preferred to be back in Australia.

When we entered the shop, a petite, very attractive woman dressed in a lime green sarong rushed from the rear of the shop. On closer inspection, she was probably only sixteen or so, and her chocolate coloured, blemish free skin, set off her jet-black eyes, her brilliant white teeth and long black hair.

'Good morning gentlemen,' she said in near perfect English. 'Welcome to our shop. Do you have an appointment, or would you prefer to study the rare beauty and value of our merchandise on display?'

'We would be delighted to inspect your wares, but later perhaps,' I said as politely as possible, then dropped my bomb. 'We have come a long way to meet with the owner of this shop; would you please let him know that his friend Les Harper is waiting to talk with him.'

Our host suddenly looked alarmed, her eyes now wide open, her eyelids blinking rapidly.

Clam too was now looking sideways at me, for I hadn't explained my intended approach. Yet, quick as a flash, Clam nodded slightly, the signal that I should proceed.

The shop attendant wheeled and bolted for the back room, from where suddenly an unpleasant and clearly agitated voice erupted; though not in English, I was otherwise certain I recognised its source.

Not thirty seconds passed before a quite well dressed, snowy haired and bespectacled white man in his mid to late sixties appeared. Trailing him with a shy expression, nothing like the confident girl who greeted us, and probably deeply embarrassed, was his shop attendant.

'So, who the fuck *are* you? You're not Les Harper!'

'And greetings to you, Archie mate. But *I am* Les Harper, I can assure you. Remember the last time we met? That time you were crawling all over a young boy no more than twelve years old. And remember who it was that persuaded the police that you were not a paedophile and should not be sent to prison? And I see you've changed your sexual preferences again.'

At this revelation, the girl gasped, placed a hand over her mouth and this time bolted for the front door. 'Go on yah dopey bitch, get out and don't come back,' Archie yelled at her.

'And you're still the same obnoxious individual; that was no way to talk to a young woman. You'd not get away with that in Australia: you sicken me, Archie.'

'But, but', Archie stammered. 'You don't look anything like the Les Harper I knew.'

'Well, get used to it,' I replied aggressively. 'It's amazing what a nose job can do. But aren't you more interested in why I'm here?'

'No, not really ... unless you want to buy something. Anyway, who's this black fella?'

'Oh, him? I thought you'd never ask. He's my personal assistant who helps me with negotiations. He can be quite persuasive: I've seen him reduce a bloke half his age to tears and begging for his life in less than five minutes. So, that's something else you'll have to get used to.'

I turned to look at Clam, who was now staring intently at Archie through hooded eyes and smiling in a maniacal manner, which even shocked me.

Archie took a quick step backwards, both arms raised in mock defence and said, 'OK, OK, Les, what the hell do you want from me?'

'Your cooperation, Archie. And if you give us what we want, you could be on an earner. Any bullshit and you'll lose both your shops. My friend here also has an excellent record of reducing buildings to ashes.

'I see that you now understand the position you're in, so Archie, please lock the front door and let's sit somewhere comfortable for a civilised chat.'

18

'I'll come straight to the point Archie, are you being blackmailed or paying protection money to anyone? Think carefully before you reply, your life will probably depend upon you telling me the truth.'

Archie recoiled in surprise and initially remained silent. As if on cue, Clam started to rise from his seat, while rather theatrically cracking the knuckles on both his hands.

Archie quickly raised his forearms in pretence of seeking protection.

Clam sat.

'Yes, as a matter of fact, I am.'

'Well, go on, elaborate, I haven't got all day,' I insisted.

'Coincidentally, an oldish Australian bloke I'd say, phoned me about three weeks ago, threatening that if I don't pay him a significant whack before the end of this month, he'll give his permission to a local gang to rob both of my shops and remove every last piece of my jewellery.'

'So, how much is he asking?' Clam interrupted. 'And did he demand that you *do not* alert the police?'

'He wants the equivalent of a hundred and fifty thousand US

dollars, or the same in uncut, non-traceable diamonds. And yes, the bastard has promised me a bullet in the head if I renege and approach the police.'

'I'm sure a wealthy and clever businessman like you Archie, can see the wisdom of complying,' I replied, somewhat sarcastically. 'But do you really know who you're dealing with?'

'I've been in this business for many years and from time to time I hear things like this sort of operation; but I've never reckoned they would target me. Look, at the moment, I can cover the cash angle, but once only. If he has a second crack at me, I'm out of Singapore for good and he won't get anything.'

Again, Clam interrupted. 'So, have you got a name for us?'

'Yes, I have. But will you keep it to yourselves?'

'We will, but only if our investigations confirm what you tell us,' I replied.

'I think it's a prick known in the trade as The Diamond Whisperer. It's rumoured he *somehow gets wind* of intended jewellery robberies—diamonds mostly—or of major international diamond transfers, then relieves the owner of their rocks before anyone's the wiser.

'I can't get my mind around why the bastard would target me?' Archie added as if talking to himself.

'It's an unhealthy ownership preoccupation which he shares with his other obsession,' I quickly assured this creep, 'and that's killing anyone who ever dobs him in, or who can recognise him through business arrangements having gone wrong. It's been estimated he's directly and indirectly responsible for more than thirty murders, including thirteen in Australia.'

'God almighty Les, what do you reckon I ought a do?'

Clam answered for me. 'Comply and keep your trap shut, then go for an extended holiday in Siberia.'

Just as Clam and I were about to leave Archie's shop, Clam asked, ever so politely. 'I say, Archie, perchance when you spoke with that Whisperer fella, did you write down the incoming phone number?'

'Why would you think I'd do that?'

'Because Archie,' Clam replied conversationally, 'you're a dope and you too are also a vengeful individual who'd never miss an opportunity to exert your mistaken overblown abilities to influence a potential adverse situation. Am I correct?'

Archie blanched visibly but had the decency to retrieve that phone number for us.

'I hope for your sake Archie that this isn't a bogus number,' Clam said, hoping I dare say, that our *friend* fully grasped the consequences of attempting any form of retribution of his own. But then, idiots always remain idiots.

* * *

IT WOULD BE an understatement to say that we left Archie in a state of anxiety, his hands were shaking, and I suspect he was about to throw up if the speed with which he ushered us from his shop and then proceeded to lock the front door behind us was any indication.

We had only walked about fifty yards away from Archie's shop when our taxi glided to a stop next to us and quietly honked to attract our attention. A surprise, yes, but a most welcome service given that the sun held quite a sting.

'To the Australian Consulate please driver,' Clam ordered politely. 'I don't suppose you have any water on board?'

'Of course, sir,' our driver replied with a smile. 'I can be there is less than fifteen minutes if you wish. There's cold water in the compartment of each side-door. Please help yourself.'

'There's no rush but thank you for keeping an eye out for us,' Clam said. 'But tell me, how on earth did you happen to be in the immediate area?'

'A fluke, sir. Though if I told you the truth, you'd never believe me. Just one of the tricks of our trade.'

19

It was unexpectedly easy to gain an audience with the High Commissioner representing Australian interests in Singapore. An affable type, seemingly very interested in our need for assistance, he eagerly read the document that Clam presented to him.

'And the nature of your request is what, specifically?' he asked judiciously.

'We believe it would greatly advance our investigation if we knew the name and address of the party registered to that phone number,' Clam replied courteously as he handed him the slip of paper provided by Archie.

'Ehhm, I must say, this sounds all very cloak-and-dagger-ish,' replied the Commissioner, 'but can you reveal to me who provided you with this phone number?'

'No,' Clam replied emphatically. 'However, I can assure you that our endeavours are of interest to both Australian and international parties, many of whom are seeking closure to multiple murders and grand theft.'

'If I may add, sir,' I interrupted, 'your forensic investigators may have access to fingerprint technology which could identify the bloke who gave us that number. It's my belief he will prove to be more than just a person of interest to Singapore authorities.'

'I understand, the matter of his identity is a local matter, which I'll address carefully with those authorities. And *I* can assure you gentlemen, that I'll use all my resources to provide you with what you need, but I can't guarantee anything until I've spoken with your people in Canberra.

'I'll see what I can do, but I'll keep this slip of paper; have you kept a record of the number?'

Clam nodded in affirmation.

'I have a fair idea where you gentlemen are staying should we need to meet again,' the commissioner said matter-of-factly as he stood signalling that our meeting was at an end.

We also rose, shook hands with our host and thanked him for his time and interest.

'Nice to meet you both,' he responded genuinely, 'but I sense the urgency of your mission, so I'd best give Canberra a call without further delay. Someone, most likely me, will revert to you asap. Cheerio.'

With that done, we made our way outside and into Singapore's dreadful humidity; but we didn't have to endure it for long, for yes, waiting at the street curb was our faithful taxi driver.

20

Back at the hotel, Clam and I quickly recounted for Leigh and Thommo, our meetings with Archie and the Australian High Commissioner. Both Australian's yet so different; one a manipulating degenerate paedophile who'd sell his mother for ten quid, the other, an honest as the day is long public servant, dedicated to serving Australia's best interests; not unlike the four of us when I think about it.

* * *

In the shade of enormous umbrellas, we sat around the hotel pool, reading newspapers, having the occasional dip, enjoying the occasional cold local beer and chatting amiably about just about anything that came to mind.

'Hey, fella's, listen to this,' Thommo suddenly uttered while chuckling to himself. Reading from his newspaper, he recited, 'where would a one-armed pirate buy a hook?'

The rest of us were left searching our brains for an answer, but before we could do so, Thommo blurted out the answer. 'In a second-hand shop of course!'

Good one Thommo!

A few seconds later, Clam added an even better tale. 'Did you hear about the dwarf psychic who broke out of prison?'

Again, before anyone could answer, Clam provided the answer. 'Yeah, well, the police are now searching for a small, medium at large.'

This evoked far more robust laughter; including that from the hotel manager who had overheard the telling of that tale as he arrived to announce that dinner would be served in the hotel's dining room. In fact, it had such a profound effect upon his sense of humour and his ability to remain standing, that Leigh had to help him back into the hotel.

When Leigh returned a few minutes later, he said, 'the poor bugger was only trying to tell us that dinner would be at eight o'clock; something special made for us by his wife and her sister; and that no formal dress is required.'

* * *

WE ARRIVED PUNCTUALLY at the hotel dining room, immediately aware that something special awaited us if the aromas that reached us were any indication. Soft Asian music was playing and the hotel manager greeted us amiably. Overhead fans rotated slowly to compliment a balmy breeze trickling into the dining room through open doors and windows.

Introductions followed; we finally learnt the manager's name, Anthony, and formally met his wife Leia, and her wheelchair bound sister Averlyn. Both welcomed us in fluent English, while offering us a choice of ice-cold tropical fruit juices and suggesting that we be seated.

A formidable table setting beckoned: a vibrant, colourful culinary scene with numerous dishes which included Hainanese chicken rice, chili crab, laksa, and nasi lemak. Those dishes were named and proudly presented by Leia and Averlyn who suggested that we all leave some space for other Singapore favourites to follow, such as kaya toast, bak kut teh, char kway teow, and satay.

To our surprise, both women joined us at the table while Anthony plied us with drinks, anything from water to whiskey.

All three of our hosts were great company and we learnt much about their lives: Averlyn's life however remained somewhat of a mystery. It transpired that she was not in fact disabled in any way whatsoever, the wheelchair was a diversion when assigned to special operations for our High Commissioner. Though exactly what she meant by *diversion* I chose not to ask. Her information did however make me realise just how far our family of international cooperation extended.

That wonderful meal and the generous company was not the only surprise of that memorable evening ... but the veiled eye contact intended to be shared only between Clam and Averlyn certainly was.

As we were retiring to our rooms, a familiar voice called out to us from the end of the corridor serving our rooms.

'I say Clam, we need to talk.'

'Commissioner!' Clam replied cheerfully. 'How nice that we meet again, and so soon. But what on earth has compelled you to join us at this late hour?'

'This!' the commissioner said as he joyfully waved a sheet of paper. 'I can't stay long; Canberra wants my earliest possible confirmation that I've delivered this to you. I'm aware you are all leaving Singapore early tomorrow, far better that you get this news now, just in case for some reason your plane departs early.

'I truly hope this helps with your investigations lads. Please let me know one day if it did.' And with that he smiled contentedly, waved to our team and departed at a jog back along the corridor.

We then quickly filed into Clam's room, all of us decidedly keen to learn what that single sheet of paper would reveal. Clam waved for us to be seated then read its contents. Having finished, he smiled, raised his eyebrows and handed the page on to me. It read, in neat concise handwriting: -

Number registered to Polish woman, according to the records she completed at check-in to manager of Dinner Plain Resort. Passport was not presented. We will speak to resort manager about this failure to follow protocol.
The name she provided was W. Kluczewski.
Age; a guess, 45-48. Attractive. Long black hair & eyes. Not the politest individual. Chip on shoulder??
Private address provided was: -
Wacław Kluczewski
ul. Zientarskiego 16 m. 41
26-615 Radom
Daughter's name: Jennie Czarnecki. Age; a guess, 7-9. Cute and polite. Maybe an authentic name, albeit from a previous marriage? Adopted? Possibly.
Info could be either a trap, or just plain stupid. Either way, pursue with caution.
We will not intrude upon your project unless requested. Too much interest may create unwanted suspicions and necessitate local authority investigations. When settled, provide updated contact details.
HT helps + GL.

I handed the note to Leigh, who read it slowly, occasionally nodding his head. He then passed it to Thommo who read it, intermittently raising his eyebrows and smiling before handing it back to Clam.

'It really is a small world,' I replied, somewhat incredulous. 'However, it's really comforting that a genuine, smart and caring team has got our back.'

'So, it's *our team* now Richard?' asked Clam with just a hint of cynicism. 'But yes, we are never short of wise counsel and physical backup when it's needed.

'Right, now Leigh, Thommo and you too Richard, I want you all to memorize the information you've just read, then let's all get some sleep.

'Make sure you pack before you hit the sack. There's no rush to be up super early. But I was thinking we should all go for a run in the park over the road and then have a swim before breakfast; that should set us up nicely for the flight ahead of us.'

Not only did we not receive a bill for our stay at that lovely hotel, but our ever-reliable taxi driver was waiting at the front door ready to engage the early airport-bound traffic.

Anthony, Leia and Averlyn (minus her wheelchair) made an effusive fuss over us, plying us with firm handshakes, hugs, kisses and offering genuine well wishes as we boarded our taxi. They would never be forgotten.

At the airport, though we again thanked the taxi driver for his faultless service, he steadfastly refused any notion that he should receive a tip. A donation towards the education of his children was, however, enthusiastically accepted.

21

———————

Our Qantas flight departed on schedule. And I must say, there was a palpable air of excitement not only in the departure waiting room, but even more so, as we filed onto the plane and buckled up.

At that time, Qantas was only the second airline flying Super Constellations west from Australia to London through Asia and the Middle East. Depending upon unexpected mechanical or engine problems, the weather, access to fuel, and political posturing's, it usually required at least two stopovers; primarily to refuel. A stewardess confided in me that there had been an instance of six forced stopovers on one most forgettable flight. She was, however, quick to reassure me that that was now most unlikely.

A most unwanted premonition flashed across my mind, that this just might be another such flight given what the tropical updrafts were inflicting upon our plane. Yet, it miraculously held together and once the cruising altitude was reached free of unexpected bumps, the flight attendants were quick to trot out a range of comforting and restorative spirits, including an eighteen-year-old Talisker single malt Scotch whisky.

About an hour later, I changed seats with Thommo to learn more about Leigh. He was welcoming, and on for a chat. I'd decided to catch up with Thommo later; we still had many hours of flying with only limited things to entertain ourselves apart from an inflight magazine ... besides I thought Thommo would probably appreciate the aisle seat from where he could better exert his charm on a very attractive blond flight attendant.

'I say mate, we've known each other for months,' I probed lightly with Leigh, 'but I still don't know your surname.'

'Actually, I don't have one to give you; that's one of our security protocols. A bit like you now being Richard, so don't be offended. Same deal with Thommo by the way. The difference is that you need a surname; Zarkas is very middle European and may assist to open a few doors that the rest of us can't.'

'No offence taken, but I noticed you've been busy writing. Anyone special?'

'Oh, this? Sort of. I do a bit of pencil sketching from time to time, portraits mostly. Here, what do think of our horny colleague?'

At first glance of the incomplete image on Leigh's sketch pad, there was absolutely no mistaking that it was Thommo!

'Mate, that's bloody good,' I replied genuinely impressed. 'Where'd you learn to do that?'

'My old man is a gifted and highly skilled professional artist; he even has his own gallery in Melbourne. Trained in Paris for a few years, so I guess his skills rubbed off on me ... just a little bit.

'Depending on Clam's plans for us, we might get to meet him. Last I heard he's in London either creating something new or lecturing.'

No sooner were the words out of Leigh's mouth than I suddenly had a creative idea of my own. 'I say Leigh,' I asked, sure to get his attention, 'instead of sketching someone who's right in front of you, could you produce a facial sketch from how I described someone to you?'

'You mean of someone, who for whatever reason, is still embedded in your memory?

'Yes, precisely.'

'That's exactly what we underwent as part of our forensics training at Duntroon, so, yes, I reckon I can produce something. There's no time like the present mate, so see what you can retrieve from that brain of yours. Take your time.'

For the next forty minutes I waffled on while Leigh's pencil darted back and forth across his sketch pad.

Unexpectedly, Leigh paused, stopped scribbling, passed his pad to me and said proudly, 'Here mate, see what yah reckon. Be frank; no bullshit.'

'Christ Almighty Leigh, that's nothing short of bloody remarkable.'

It was now my turn to pause, for despite the passage of thirty or so years, The Diamond Whisperer was staring straight back at me!

'I'm gobsmacked mate, but tell me, could you do a second sketch of that same bloke for me, but thirty years on? You know, what he might look like today.'

'Geeze, you don't want much do yah? but yes, I'll give it a go.'

Nearly an hour passed before Leigh stopped working. 'There you go mate,' Leigh said, albeit less enthusiastically than he did about his first sketch.

'Realistic enough for you Richard?

'Hang on, are you feeling OK mate? You look like you've just been sprung in the hayshed with the farmer's daughter.'

Before I could speak, I experienced an annoying flush of déjà vu.

'Mate, this is really good work. And do you know what? Somewhere in the recent history, I reckon I've seen this face.

'I'll be back in a second, I want to show your drawings to Clam.'

With some difficulty I extracted myself from my window seat, crawled across Leigh's legs and staggered across the aisle to where Clam was fast asleep in his tilted-back chair.

'Excuse me mate,' I said, feeling guilty as I gently thumped Clam on his shoulder. I was going to say, *this could be important*, but I swear, in less than a blink, Clam was wide awake and on the verge of delivering a fist to my unprotected face.

'Easy son,' I begged quickly, finally able to say my piece. 'Clam, this could be important, and I wouldn't wear a black eye as easily as you. There's no rush, but would you mind having a look at these and tell me what you think?'

'Sorry Richard, I was on walkabout, back in Arnhem Land. Show me what you've got there.'

A minute or two passed as Clam studiously examined Leigh's sketches.

'This here older bloke,' Clam said calmly while tapping a finger onto the second sheet of paper. He'd be one of those bastards who used us for target practice back in Swift's Creek. So, who's the young bloke?'

'It's the same bloke only thirty years younger; at least, that's how I remember him, so *I* reckon that's our man; that goddam Diamond Whisperer fella!'

'Tell Leigh I'm impressed. Fingers crossed this will help us snare that bastard before he kills anyone else, but get back to your seat, lunch is about to be served.'

'I have to say, this is most unexpected and mighty encouraging,' Thommo added after he got to see those sketches, after lunch. 'But it's still circumstantial, not factual.'

'You're correct, but it's better than what we had just a few hours ago,' Clam said with a wry smile. 'And I bet Canberra will be suitably impressed with Leigh's creativeness.'

Back in my seat, I said to Leigh, 'Mate, keep these sketches safe, they may prove to be very useful.

'But tell me, do you reckon your dad might have crossed paths with the so-called Diamond Whisperer, for he also had a penchant for great artwork?'

'That settles it Richard, we'll just have to find him and ask. As soon as we've had lunch, I'll get into Clam's ear and see if he agrees.

'I reckon you can bank on it.'

* * *

IT WAS an enormous relief to finally hear the captain announcing that we were due to arrive in London in about twenty-five minutes.

Our second stopover at Damascus in Syria had been much anticipated in terms of getting some fresh air and exercise, but our expectations had been dashed. Apparently due to some ongoing civilian unrest, evidenced by the number of heavily armed soldiers wandering around the exterior of the terminal, we were banned from leaving the plane and were therefore confined to our seats.

The refuelling process seemed to go on forever and conditions within the plane became hot and foul. Add to that the screaming of a few babies, dopey passengers arguing with stressed stewardesses over being unlawfully denied their right to smoke, and the discomfort of out-of-service toilets, you can no doubt understand the relief that followed once we were again airborne. Yet, we still had to endure at least another eight or so hours of confinement wherein uncompromising engine noise sought to curtail the ability to hold a meaningful conversation of any duration.

On the other hand, you can perhaps get a sense of our further frustration when the captain announced an "unfortunate delay" due to thick fog having moved in to completely blanket the Heathrow Airport. The solution: we would fly on to Manchester where the fog had been replaced by light rain. Another delay followed, another hour of our lives squandered.

* * *

MANCHESTER AIRPORT STAFF recognised how tired we were and kindly whisked us away to a nearby multistorey hotel. Within minutes of checking in, we were shown to our respective rooms: bugger the cost, that could be sorted out later.

22

———

I woke at least twenty-four hours later, bursting for a pee, and famished.

But there were other things on my mind. I'd been hoping my previous multiple air travel experiences, though several years ago, would somehow immune me from jetlag, but I was wrong, and to be honest I suffered from varying degrees of wooziness for at least the next three days. In fact, none of us fared any better, which was of very little consolation. However, hats off to those pilots who can somehow front up for long-haul return flights within just thirty-six hours, apparently unaffected.

To my surprise, when we finally assembled for lunch in the hotel's dining room, Clam wasted no time to explain to us that he had already been in touch with Canberra and had convinced them we needed a few days to recover ... but I was not surprised he didn't explain to them the full extent of his intended plan, particularly for the next day or so, other than that we would need a reliable vehicle and visas to complement our passports for our journey to Warsaw, Poland's capital city.

Canberra agreed to cover our extended hotel costs (compliments of the Australian Consulate in London) but they needed a few days to organise our documentation. That suited us perfectly, for we didn't fancy trooping about in the unrelenting cold, windy and wet weather. Besides, Clam had a specific plan in mind, to be best discussed privately, indoors and in comfort ... which we later learnt included a gym and sauna.

* * *

HAVING COMPLETED A HEARTY LUNCH, we assembled in Clam's room.

'OK. let's focus,' Clam demanded forcefully, but without spite. 'Interrupt only if necessary. There'll be plenty of time later to raise anything I've overlooked, or if you want to suggest a better approach.

'Our primary goal is unchanged; to which we are tasked to complete, whatever it takes. Which implies from this point forward I believe our lives are potentially on the line. If any of you want to reconsider your previous commitment, now's the time to do so. There'll be no recriminations.'

Nice one Clam, I thought, *maybe I should have stuck to growing rubber trees.*

But someone still wants me killed and I now had an appetite to even things up.

'I'm in,' I said, to which followed a unanimous response.

'Thank you,' Clam replied to each of us separately, nodding slightly as he did so in what I interpreted as the cementing of an unspoken, special bond.

'As I was going to say,' Clam continued, 'there are two closely related issues involved. First, the murder of more than thirty innocent Australian farmers and a variety of European folk; and second, the recovery of an enormous quantity of diamonds stolen when on Australian soil.

'Those murders can still be contested in court, however, what information we have with respect to the stolen diamonds is fundamentally hearsay. Intuitively, however, I believe that, if we can find the murderer in question, we'll have found The Diamond Whisperer ... and subsequently we'll find those missing diamonds.

'Now let's recap on what we do know. For example, I've worked with the Belgian Criminal Investigations Police Department with who I still have close personal and professional friendships. I got shot in the backside while on duty, as I recall telling you, however, that operation resulted in a few significant arrests. Regrettably the mastermind still evaded us. Interestingly, that operation was a set up to snare him at an elaborately conducted and very private auction of rare, and very valuable artworks.

Leigh's head shot up!

'No one has ever found those missing diamonds, and nobody has any idea where they are. Conjecture has it that someone must move those diamonds regularly, though that sounds impractical. So, is there a link between the stolen artwork and the stolen diamonds? And if so, where are they hidden?

'It's also interesting that despite the on-going work of the Belgian police, they have not yet located anyone who has purchased uncut diamonds or valuable artwork. Which means, I believe, that our charming friend has in fact moved or relocated his hordes of both items. Based upon our experience back home, when we snatched Richard from the Dinner Plains resort, my money is on Poland, for that's where we not only have a name, but where that person may live.

'I also have a theory relating to that artwork. I suspect it has possibly overstretched his ability to keep things out of the public eye, but the woman whose name we have, may be either his wife, or his de facto wife. So, logically, if we can locate and arrest Miss Wactaw Kluczewski, we'll also stand a bloody good chance of trapping our man. He's bound to slip up eventually.

'Thanks to Leigh's remarkable memory for detail and his brilliant sketches we now probably have the best shot at arresting our so-called Diamond Whisperer. However, Leigh, I'm definitely not accusing your father of being somehow involved.'

Leigh nodded his acceptance.

At this point, there was suddenly a knock on the door of Clam's room, just a few firm taps. 'Ah, at last, that'll be our afternoon tea if I'm not mistaken.'

* * *

STRONG COFFEE and luscious cream-filled sponge cake, topped with dark chocolate no less, proved the perfect foil to the intensity of Clam's dissertation. Little was said between us, however; we were all no doubt mulling over what Clam had just delivered.

After essential toilet visits, once again Clam took the floor.

'Right, please stay focused. As I've said before, my lovely wife, Gerde, was murdered not long after that sting failed to nail the mastermind. Did she die because she got to see that person's face? Probably, I suspect. Of course, I have a deep personal reason to succeed in capturing this maniac, but I assure you all that this does not mean I hold a conflict of interest which could jeopardise the task ahead: I just want this bastard arrested and put out of action once and for all.

'And, more recently, perhaps because our man is feeling the heat of ongoing multi-national investigations, Richard here, may still have been considered a high enough risk to be able to identify him ... and therefore likewise needed to be eliminated. I think we've covered that eventuality. We got to Les in the nick of time and he, Les Harper, has effectively disappeared for ever. Not even his mother could now identify Richard as her son. We therefore hold a very strong card that Richard would be able to recognise our man.

'We also have the unconditional support of manpower resources if, and as required, compliments of the Polish, Belgian and Dutch Criminal Investigations teams: all trusted friends of mine. However, more importantly, we have the overriding authority to call the shots regarding whatever action we need to take, when and how.

'But what still frustrates me is that we still have no idea how our homicidal friend got wind of the plans to transport that massive consignment of diamonds from the Netherlands to a supposed safe, remote refuge in Australia.'

Clam finally called it quits and asked for questions.

'I've got just one Clam,' I replied, 'what's next?'

'First, we need to get to London and locate Leigh's dad. And then Amsterdam, then Bruges, and then to Warsaw … roughly in that order.

'Please be ready for an early departure tomorrow morning. I've arranged for breakfast to be served at seven o'clock, and we leave at seven forty-five.

'Hang about boys, I almost forgot something,' Clam said quickly and somewhat embarrassed I suspect.

'Which was?' I enquired respectfully.

'We've got to do some serious thinking about how our man could possibly have remained out of site for so long.'

23

As we strode from our hotel, two casually dressed non-threatening looking gentlemen approached us. 'Which one of you is Clam?'

'That'd be me,' Clam replied in an equally non-threatening manner. 'Who wants to know, pray tell? My name's Callum; Clam to my friends.'

That a black man was our spokesman, seemed not to offend either chap, who both quickly came forward to introduce themselves and presented their respective ID badges. 'Your transport gentlemen, unfortunately the most decrepit of the two parked at the curb,' said the eldest bloke.

His companion, a lad in his mid-twenties, about Thommo's age, was quick to add, 'she might have a few years on her but she's jolly reliable and might surprise you if you need to put your foot down, like.

'The tank's full and there's a five-litre tank of extra fuel in the boot, along with a two-litre bottle of engine oil. Standard tools are in there as well.'

'And here's a legit driver's license,' the older bloke chimed in. 'It's a special document meant for use only by authorised Government Public Servants; it should keep you lot out of trouble.'

'That's damn kind of your government,' Clam replied courteously, 'but have those same people supplied the road maps I requested?'

'In spades, Clam,' the older official replied happily. 'On the back seat, in separate brown paper bags labelled by country, along with your visas for each country you've nominated.

'I'm also obliged to let you know that the other four boxes on the back seat contain handguns and ammunition: standard London police issue. It was deemed you might find them useful, but they are only to be used to protect yourselves ... and must be surrendered when your mission is complete.'

'You boys have thought of everything; your help is very gratefully accepted. We can't possibly fail now, though a bit of good luck along the way just might be helpful.' With that said, two sets of car keys were handed to Clam. All round handshakes followed along with mutual and genuine well wishes.

'London in sixty-five; take the M6 from here and then join the M1 at Leeds,' the young bloke shouted as he waved a final farewell.

24

With Thommo as the dedicated driver, the trip to London was fast, comfortable and distinctly different to most of the Australia with which we were familiar. Multi-lane motorways, plus the sheer size of Manchester and Leeds, and then later, the row upon row of housing commission buildings as we converged upon the outskirts of London, caused me to reflect upon how lucky we were back at home, despite a persistent threat of bush fires, floods and drought.

'Nah, could never live here,' I heard Clam mumble to himself on more than one occasion, as if voicing the thoughts flashing through my mind. In fairness though, well grassed and stocked paddocks, stands of large trees, period styled farmhouses, quaint, yet imposing chalet style, thatched roof cottages set back from the motorway and hedged fence lines, combined to create an appealing sense of order and charm ... in stark contrast to the high density living of those over-whelmingly large, odorous and drab cities.

As planned, when we were about thirty miles from London, Thommo pulled into a petrol station come roadside cafe; not for fuel, but to give Leigh a chance to locate his father. There was no guarantee he was in London, but he had become an important person of interest; and try we must to locate him.

Two coffees and a few slices of buttered raisin bread later, Leigh looked up from the telephone book he'd been studying and said triumphantly, 'I reckon I've got him! There can't be too many P S Marshalls', Consignment Artist and Fine Artwork Trader's, in London ... and this one's at Victoria Station, smack bang in Central London.'

Leigh immediately commandeered the cafe's public phone, while I copied down the details Leigh had circled in the phone book.

It wasn't long before the look on Leigh's face changed from one of doubt to jubilation, his vigorous thumbs up and beaming smile leaving the rest of us in no doubt of his success. His conversation lasted less than five minutes, during which time he frantically scribbled notes, presumably directions of where we could meet.

'Got him?' Clam enquired rather needlessly, intentionally giving Leigh the opening he needed to fill us in.

'Yep, and by the way, my dad's name is Peter Stevenson Marshall, Pete to family and his friends.

'However, there are a few problems. First, he only has room enough for one guest; lucky that his girlfriend is at her home in Paris. Second, there's bugger all local accommodation.'

'Or parking for that matter, I suppose,' Thommo interrupted.

'Actually, parking won't be a problem, dad has an unused garage space. Accommodation won't be too much of a problem; he's currently securing that for you three: you'll only be ten minutes away. I'll stay with him tonight, but taxis are everywhere, so getting to and from your hotel should be a breeze.'

'Bloody well-done Leigh,' Clam replied. 'I'm sure we're all looking forward to meeting your father. But I insist, please let him know we're on a tight program and that I'd greatly appreciate it if he would devote the majority of tomorrow to answering some critical questions.'

'Don't worry, I'll make it happen,' Leigh replied confidently.

* * *

As Thommo drove on, he did so under the gathering stress of our well-intentioned but occasional conflicting directions. And to make matters worse for him, it started to rain so hard it was impossible to read any street signs. Yet Thommo soldiered on, only once getting us completely lost.

When Thommo eventually slowed and then stopped in front of our destination, a clean shaven, oldish looking bloke with a large curling moustache and a shock of long white hair, walked briskly from an open garage space, out into the rain, and gestured with a flourish that Thommo should drive straight inside without delay.

'OK lads, out you get,' Peter ordered cheerfully as he shook whatever rain had accumulated on his three-quarter length anorak. 'Go up those stairs but mind your noggins as the staircase changes direction halfway up.

'I thought you'd never get here, just as well it wasn't raining from the nor-east.'

Father and son embraced, then introductions followed.

Peter was a likeable type; about my age I guessed. He was also on for a chat, but as soon as the rain eased, he called a taxi. 'If I'm not mistaken,' he said putting an end to his inquisitiveness, 'I'll expect you all back here no sooner than nine o'clock tomorrow. You can easily find your own way down to the garage. Your taxi will probably already be there waiting. But please, don't forget to close the roller shutter door; just press the big red mushroom shaped button once only. You can't miss it, it's inside the garage, on the right-hand side. And please, don't hang around for it to close or you'll get locked in.'

25

———————

The next morning, Clam, Thommo and I had a typical Pommy breakfast (not recommended to become habitual, unless massive weight gain issues hold no fear for you), then we grabbed a taxi to Peter Marshall's studio apartment.

Leigh and his father were standing together in the garage opening and were quick to greet us we exited from our taxi. Bugger it! It was my turn to pay.

'I say, Clam,' Leigh immediately sprang into action, 'would it bugger up your plans if Thommo and I were to pay a visit to the Queen. According to that taxi driver Buckingham Palace is only a short walk from Victoria Station. We can be there and back here within an hour.'

'And besides,' I said in support, 'opportunities like this don't crop up too often, eh?'

'You've got an hour and a half,' Clam graciously agreed. 'Give my regards to our Royal Highness.'

'I second that,' Peter added, 'but don't feed her dogs, they're ferocious and they bite.

'And when you get back, there's a small black button mounted on a brass plate; press it and I'll come down and let you in.'

That said, Leigh and Thommo bolted from the garage, heading for Victoria Station.

As it transpired, their absence proved to be quite fruitful.

* * *

PETER WAS quick to ply us with tea, black, not sweetened, a pleasant enough change from coffee, during which time Clam steered our conversation towards Clam and me.

'I say Peter, what can you tell me and Richard about those two lads? Apart from being invaluable national assets, they have a close bond. Like brothers, always got each other's backs covered.'

'Actually Clam, I don't know much about Thommo, but I do recall Leigh once told me he grew up being fatherless. Apparently, his old man had trouble financing Thommo's child support and rather than paying a considerable cash catch-up settlement, and because he was on track for a jail sentence ... he very effectively disappeared.'

'And that, Peter, is not too dissimilar to what happened with the bloke we're looking for,' I added casually. 'But that's probably just a coincidence.'

'Oh yes, I also believe Thommo had some very good luck along the way. After his mother also took off unannounced, and to God only knows where, he was immediately adopted by a compassionate immigrant Dutch family and became master Thomas Van Orsouw.

The only other thing I know about Thommo is that he and Leigh were from very different parts of Australia; in Thommo's case, from Margaret River in Western Australia, and in Leigh's case, from suburban Melbourne. I do know they were both recruited in the same year to attend The Duntroon Military College. However, from that point on, getting any information from either of them or about their type of work, has been like getting blood from a stone.'

'And so that should be,' Clam interjected without malice. 'You should know that both lads have turned out to be exceptionally capable men, and that both were screened very carefully before entering Duntroon. Nevertheless Peter, your information will be kept confidential.

'And what about your son, Leigh, what can you tell us?'

'His mother and I didn't always see eye to eye; however, Leigh had always been our focus. He was an only child, but he handled losing his mother to cancer extremely well. We openly discussed everything, and he embraced living alone when my work took me overseas more often where the main market for my paintings existed. And I think meeting Thommo at Duntroon did him a lot of good.

Anyway, it's so comforting that we still get on extremely well, and I'm extremely proud of his achievements. And even though he hasn't met my lovely French girlfriend, Francine, I know they've spoken at length a few times on the phone.'

During the previous ten or so minutes, Clam had taken to glancing at his watch. 'Look, Peter, it's time we broadened our discussion, but I want those two involved from this point on, so I suggest we have a break until they return.

Those words were barely out of Clam's mouth than a hidden buzzer alerted Peter that he had visitors. 'I'll go and see who's there. I bet it's them.'

As the three men filed back into Peter's lounge, Peter was making quite a fuss about the boxes Leigh and Thommo were carrying. 'Bloody hell boys, you didn't have to do this, but wow ... chocolate and rum, and orange and passionfruit sponge cakes with stacks of cream filling no less.

'No queue necessary men, just grab a plate and help yourselves. Seconds are not only welcome but mandatory.'

An hour later, Clam encouraged Peter to again take the lead, it being obvious he was keen to contribute to our mission, though at that time he had no idea how that would be of any use.

'Over the years, my ego, and a fair bit of luck somehow complimented my flair for creating half decent paintings. I gradually gained a respectable reputation and learnt much about how the international art world functions.

'As my reputation grew, so did my wealth. In fact, I'm a very wealthy bloke according to my solicitor but currently I have no idea exactly how wealthy.'

This resulted in looks of bewilderment between us and a few raised eyebrows.

'How so?' Clam asked.

'Well, to give you an idea, during the last annual financial year, I paid more to ensure my unsold art than I've ever before paid, combined, for all the insurance I've ever paid! And that was more than five hundred quid!'

I wasn't the only one to gasp out loud.

'And, of course, it was also costing me an arm and a leg to pay for storage for my creations. And intuitively, I never felt the level of security was as robust as it could and should have been.

'However, my solicitor and life-long friend suspected I was being taken for a ride on both counts, so he made enquiries on my behalf and discovered that he should set up a Swiss Bank account for me. Apparently, not only do they provide guaranteed security and storage conditions, but their service fees are not something I couldn't afford; besides another element of Swiss banks is that they are expert at minimizing tax.

'Anyway, another fact of life emerged at that time. One can't live forever, and I'd not made a contingency plan to ensure that my sole beneficiaries, Leigh of course, and his sister Rebecca, must have their fifty-fifty entitlement legally secured.

'That sounds easy enough, but it took several one-on-one meetings behind a thick glass window with a Swiss Bank representative; an old bloke, Mr Smith, friendly enough, though I don't believe that was his real name. It was only possible to arrange meetings with him on specific days, his reason being that he was responsible for the management of seven bank agency offices in the Warsaw region.'

'Hang on a second Peter, before you press on mate,' Clam interrupted politely. 'You did just say Warsaw?'

'Oh, yes, I lived in Warsaw for about two years. A nice place to work; the ambient light in the late afternoon resonated with me. I think some of my best work was completed there.'

'Very interesting Peter,' Clam said, 'but did you deposit all of your work at that Swiss Bank Agency?'

'Yes, I did, for I was assured their complexes throughout Europe all had remarkably high security systems and storage condition credentials, and the documentation they required, which included the formal nomination of my two kids as beneficiaries was handled very professionally.'

'But did you get to witness where your artwork was to be stored? I asked in a measured, though pointed tone.

'Well, no,' Peter replied, suspecting now that our questioning had gone up a tad.

'Part of their security protocols included utilising several different storage locations. No employee at any facility is ever told where precious items are accommodated.'

'Do you reckon you could identify that bloke, that Mr Smith?

'Yes, I think so, why?'

'Well, would you please have a close look at this sketch that Leigh produced for us a few days ago,' Clam replied calmly as he handed over the subject drawing. 'Do you know who this is?'

'Nah, I don't know that person,' Peter replied, shaking his head.

'Then what about this bloke?' Clam said with a bit more enthusiasm as he passed Leigh's second sketch over to Peter.

'Oh, Christ yes! That's the Mr Smith I met! I'm absolutely bloody certain!'

Jubilation erupted among our team, arm's pumping the air and calls of "yes", "you've finally slipped up you prick" and "we've got you now" rang out around Peter's lounge room.

Meanwhile, Peter stood fixated and looked totally nonplussed. But when some normality returned, he asked, albeit somewhat irritably, 'what the hell's going on? What've I said to get you lot so goddam excited?'

'Sit down and relax mate,' Clam said warmly,' believe it or not, but you may have just provided the means of solving this case. Let me explain why what you've just said, is so bloody important.

'We've known for some time that a Polish woman of interest

resides in Warsaw, and we have that address. You've just told us that a bloke of interest, most likely a murderer and international thief with a penchant for stealing diamonds and high art, has also been suspected to have been a resident of Warsaw. There is, by our estimation, a very good possibility that those two cohabit.

'So, if we can arrest them simultaneously, there's a damn good chance we'll be able to recover not only many billions of stolen diamonds and return them to their rightful owners, but also recover your unsold artwork, which we can safely assume you would have never seen again. And, regrettably, which we may never recover.'

'And that then, my friends, 'Peter replied, his brains no doubt still spinning, 'is one hell of a coincidence.'

'Maybe not,' Clam replied, 'there's still the possibility that we've fallen into an elaborate trap, but no wonder nobody's been able to get a lead on this bloke; perfectly anonymous, seldom ever in public, the keeper of untold riches, and any amount of money always available to get other people to carry out his murderous biddings. And to think it even remotely possible that he's been hiding right under our bloody noses for decades and has somehow deceived a highly regarded Swiss Bank.'

26

____

'Time is still of the essence,' Clam announced before we finally called it a day.

'We must get to Poland asap, but the plan I'm visualising means that I must re-engage personally with my former crime investigation colleagues in Holland and Belgium. I'll need their permission to be able to call upon their operatives for assistance if, and when necessary.

'However, I don't have similar contacts in Poland, so I'll need Canberra to pave the way for us. All up, I think we'll need a minimum fourteen extra bodies, two per bank agency.

'So the next question is, do we travel by car, or fly?'

'The car will give us flexibility,' Thommo ventured his advice, 'and we can share the driving load. Plus, we won't have to explain to border police why we're all technically armed, because our guns and ammo will be so beautifully hidden.'

'All agreed then, we travel by car?' Clam replied to the showing of three raised hands. 'We'll be back here at seven-thirty tomorrow morning. Leigh, would you please have our car warmed up and ready to hit the road?'

* * *

THE DRIVE to Dover was uneventful and pleasant, normal I suppose for this time of year: clear blue sky with just a hint of light cloud, quite balmy and apparently with the world at peace ... except for the frustration of some erratic traffic.

* * *

UPON OUR ARRIVAL AT DOVER, we had to wait about an hour before the loading of our car onto the hovercraft cross-channel transport service to Calais; a great opportunity to relax with a cuppa and enjoy the sun's late morning warmth, and to embrace the sharp ozone tang wafting over us from the ocean.

Regrettably, our anticipated peace and quiet was soon disrupted. A bloke dressed in a bedraggled and filthy navvies uniform and carrying a "make do" walking stick of cut timber about six feet long, staggered and then stopped to stare at us. He was clearly somewhat *Brahms and Liszt.*

'Yah lazy pricks,' our visitor mouthed off, completely unprovoked. 'Why dohne yhes get orf yah fat arses an' do some work?'

As quick as a flash, Clam put down his mug, and replied cheerfully, 'And a good day to you sir, but have you forgotten something?'

'Like what, yah dopey black bastard?'

'Well, you could start with using some manners,' Clam replied calmly as he rose from his seat.

'I'll get this, he's twice your size Clam,' Thommo quickly interrupted, while placing his hand firmly upon Clam's shoulder.

'No, this is my problem, and I'll sort things out. Besides, you heard him, he just needlessly insulted my parentage.'

Thommo shrugged his shoulder, released Clam and resumed his seat.

With no further ado, Clam and our unfriendly visitor approached each other, both stopping when about four feet apart.

'Tis you as what needs tah be a bit smarter about what yah 'ave tah say.'

'Is that right boyo? Well, we obviously disagree but would you please remove your stinking body from our presence. But before you do so I'd like an apology from you for questioning my birthright. You see, I know both my parents, and both are proud to be black. But I doubt that you can remember who both your parents are.'

That did it, the navvy snarled savagely, raised his impromptu walking stick and swung it backwards before launching into an ill-considered attack upon Clam. Not halfway through his forward swing, the weapon of choice somehow magically disappeared from his grip and was on its way over the roof of the wharf-side cafe, in front of which the rest of us sat in disbelief and anticipation of what might now follow.

I'd previously witnessed how fast Clam could move; I'd never forget how quickly he'd moved on the plane, from being asleep to being ready to punch my lights out! On this occasion, he took two quick steps forward, grabbed the end of that walking stick nearest to him and reefed it from his attacker's grip. Using the momentum of the stick, Clam pivoted and flung it over his shoulder out of harm's way. Quite a fantastic performance really, but it didn't top the expression on the drunk's face as his bewildered gaze followed the stick's trajectory.

'I do hope you have some kind of medical insurance boyo, because you're going to need it if you don't apologise!' Clam continued to bait his foe.

'No way! 'ere, cop this instead!' yelled our misguided friend as he prepared to launch his right fist at Clam's unprotected head.

I've seen a few fist fights during the past years, but I'd never seen anyone strike as quickly as Clam did on this occasion. As he ducked, his own right fist slammed into the side of his foe's rib cage. We all heard the contact of Clam's *whack*, and that of a simultaneous sharp cracking sound, presumably that of a rib or two breaking under the power of that blow. Bloody amazing, given Clam was then in his forties.

Within a second, Clam's foe was on his knees, now totally bewildered and unable to decide what was best; to beg for help or try to somehow breathe but realising neither was possible. Since either action obviously didn't appeal to him, he toppled over, groaning loudly as he hit the wharf's unforgiving deck.

Unbeknown to us, this pantomime had been observed by a member of the local police force who was now ambling towards the scene.

'Well, well gentlemen, that was something to behold,' he said, bemused as we were. 'However, I'd suggest that you all make yourselves scarce. I'll deal with this now.'

Not wanting to disobey the officer's prudent advice we were quickly out of our seats and ready to leg it.

'Hang about lads,' the friendly officer advised, chuckling to himself as he did so.

'Off the record like but did you gentlemen see the look on that poor bastard's face just before he hit the deck. No? Well, I did ... it was as if he'd just received a tabasco enema.'

We arrived back at our car still laughing at the officer's fine sense of humour, just as the ferry master was announcing it was time to board the hovercraft.

27

Crossing the English Channel was two things: noisy and amazingly smooth given the surrounding ocean's surface chop.

Our planned road-trip to Warsaw was off to a good start but over the following six days, our car received a fair workout.

Though our mission was not a sight-seeing holiday, it was impossible to ignore the beauty of western and central Europe.

Border police were generally amiable types, none of whom took it upon themselves to search our car. However, it became increasingly obvious the further East we trekked that our visas seemed to gain more attention.

Much of the scenery was blessed with fertile farming pasture, clear running snowmelt rivers and dense forests. It was also noticed how the preferred housing architectural styles changed so quickly from country to country. But make no bones about it, the Alps, Pyrenees, Urals and Carpathian Mountains hold views never to be forgotten, though all of them at times challenged our driving skills, particularly where heavy snow drifts and icy road surfaces converged.

Upon arrival in Bruges, Clam made a point to visit some friends with whom he had previously worked. All were much older than

Clam, but all remembered him with affection. Those meetings were private affairs and only lasted for an hour or so.

However, Clam's meeting with Gerde's aging parents went for nearly four hours which included a visit to the cemetery where "their wonderful Gerde" had been buried. Clam later confessed that he experienced an amazing feeling of empathy which radiated from that old couple as the three of them stood, arms linked, beside Gerde's grave. His confession included tears which slid from his eyes, descended to his chin and then fell onto the great slab of granite now protecting the one true love of his life.

28

———————

Having arrived in Warsaw, Clam immediately sought and obtained a meeting with the Chief of Police, during which we gave him a heads up of who we were, and of our objectives. Notwithstanding that Clam had also presented Canberra's Letter of Introduction, he also appealed to this officer to further validate our bona fides with his counterparts in Bruges and Amsterdam.

From that point on, his cooperation was absolute and first class. He immediately assigned a large meeting room at his station to serve as the base for our operations and then guided us to a nearby hotel, enabling us to casually check-in and park our car in an off-road lockable garage.

When we arrived back at our base at about eight thirty the next morning, with Clam striding purposefully ahead, we were soon dumbfounded to find fifteen men, all dressed in plain clothes and seated around our huge table which dominated the room ... plus two German Shepherd sniffer dogs!

These were all undercover police officers, both friend and former workmates of Clam from his time serving in Bruges, Amsterdam, Paris and Krakow all stood in genuine respect of Clam, and, would you believe, they all started clapping him.

I'm sure Clam was initially a wee bit overwhelmed, but he soon regained his composure. Smiling broadly, his arms raised and waving happily, he set off to work the room. I didn't catch everything he had to say to his friends, but I did hear him emphasising how honoured he was that they had made it to Warsaw so quickly to attend this deployment. And I can tell you; he lavished great thanks upon the Senior Polish officer for his contribution in getting everyone together at such short notice. At this point, I also had a flush of pride in Clam, for just doing his job.

About half an hour later, several large pots of steaming hot coffee, mugs, milk jugs and trays of traditional Polish Babka cakes, Makowiec, a type of poppy seed roll, and Mazurek, a flat sweet cake, were all suddenly delivered to our room ... compliments of the uniformed police at the station.

But all good things must come to an end, that event being both memorable and comforting knowing how those volunteers were so damn committed to Clam ... and the rest of his Aussie team of course.

'Gentlemen!' Clam called loudly as he vigorously tapped his coffee mug with a spoon to attract everyone's attention. 'First, would somebody please close and lock the doors.'

That which followed over the next three hours was emphatic: nothing was left to chance; the substance of our undertaking was thoroughly and professionally thrashed out; it's implementation to begin at noon the next day.

Two men were assigned to an address of each registered Swiss Bank's office; their roles being to observe and make any arrest they deemed necessary. The only exception to this was, that at the wanted woman's address, three officers would be required because a back laneway provided three possible approaches to the rear of her house.

How quickly things had changed; the almost blurred days of travelling, and of relaxation had suddenly been replaced by a pressing realisation; it was time to act.

* * *

THE FOLLOWING morning was not only filled with genuine excitement, but a sense of determination.

Having synchronised our watches, each team travelled to their allocated address. At a pre-agreed time, a single team member would each simultaneously enter their assigned bank office. The second team member would be there as backup if their colleague failed to exit within a specific time.

The primary role of the first team member was to confirm whether the person in the front office was recognisable as The Diamond Whisperer, from Leigh's sketch.

It transpired that five of the bank's offices were closed, no lights were on, and each front door was securely shut, albeit displaying a 'Normal Opening Hours' notice adhered to the rear of the door's glass window panel.

One Bank office was not a bank but had obviously become a thriving bakery.

However, Thommo was in luck. He immediately recognised the old bloke behind the glass half-height, customer counter screen, even though he was seated behind a desk positioned about four feet behind that front counter.

Thommo had immediately drawn his gun and was about to vault over that counter screen to effect what he thought would be an easy arrest, but suddenly there was an extremely loud *bang and a whoosh* of escaping high pressure air. Almost instantaneously, a blur of movement followed as a third screen was hydraulically slammed into a ceiling slot, thereby totally isolating Thommo.

That screen had somehow been secretly activated by our suspect and had there not been a slight delay by The Diamond Whisperer in doing so, Thommo would almost certainly have been crushed ... and killed.

Regardless, Thommo still fired but to no avail, that rising screen was obviously bullet proof, and easily deflected his bullet. The Diamond Whisperer had then quickly exited the front office through a sturdy steel side-door which clanked loudly as it was slammed shut, thus denying Thommo a second shot or any other means of following. Perhaps had a sniffer dog been with him, that may not have been the case.

At the wanted woman's house, my assigned backup men stormed inside and arrested her, there being absolutely no doubt who she was. She was immediately handcuffed, subjected to a brisk body search then taken back to our base, fingerprinted and formally charged and then locked into a cell.

Meanwhile, I had the unenviable job of collecting her daughter from school and conveying her to a secured childcare centre. Surprisingly, when I advised her of her mother's arrest, I was pretty sure that lovely young girl shrugged in relief and smiled.

Our epic project was rapidly concluding, yet surprisingly I was left with mixed feelings. Would our adversary no longer be a threat to anyone, or not? I think we all hoped he'd just disappear. Clam had done a masterful job of leading, organising and implementing this search, but there was no mistaking his disappointment and profound frustration at this outcome.

* * *

UNBEKNOWN TO US, once darkness fell following our failed sting, someone wearing a Bluey style worker's jacket, jeans, work boots, a baseball cap and a small backpack emerged from a private garage four streets away from where Thommo had almost snared our target.

That information came to us via an observant and community minded prostitute. In her witness statement, she believed that she was perfectly located to identify that person, being no more than thirty yards away. The ambient light of that scene, viewed from her position, was still higher than she expected, and had sworn by the accuracy of her details. She also confessed that as she continued to attend to her client's wishes on her side the street, that their exertions could not be witnessed.

Coincidently, about an hour later, a taxi driver was found by the Polish traffic control police, slumped over his steering wheel and with the car's horn blaring.

But, as luck would have it, that taxi driver, despite having been stabbed multiple times, lived just long enough to identify The Diamond Whisperer from Leigh's sketches. By the reaction from the sniffer dogs, there was little doubt about who else had been in that taxi.

An all points search was carried out over the ensuing week but no person fitting that description was ever located.

29

Accepting the reality that we'd done as much as we could at this point, it was time to wrap up this deployment and make plans for our return to Canberra.

The following night we met for a celebratory dinner with our newfound friends and international allies. Getting drunk was not a priority, but a great time was had by all.

And so, the next day our team of volunteers dispersed for their respective homes with our genuine thanks.

Though Clam was duty bound to return to Canberra to provide a full report, he clearly had something on his mind: Singapore and Averlyn, that attractive, intriguing, and supposedly wheelchair bound woman.

Leigh decided to stay in London with his father, Peter, who was hell bent on arranging an important family meeting with Leigh's sister, and to then "play the tourist" for a few weeks before heading back to Australia.

As for me, well for months now I'd had that lovely woman, Joan, on my mind ... the one who'd been instrumental in my transformation from Les Harper to Richard Zarkas. It therefore seemed fitting I should also return to Canberra to see what a future with her might bring. But Joan wasn't the only girl on my mind ... I was certain there'd be room in our lives for young Jennie. But first things first I reminded myself.

Thommo had somehow found time to strike up what I suspect was a mutually consensual friendship with a very attractive female police constable who worked at the Warsaw Police Station which had become our investigations base.

At that stage, three days after our investigations had been exhausted, Clam, Thommo and I were having a farewell beer at our hotel bar to kill some time before our transport arrived, when suddenly a waiter ran up to us and said, 'Mr Clam, there is phone call for you. You can take call in lobby; please follow me.'

'Clam speaking,' I heard him say calmly, 'how can I help you?'

I can be nosy sometimes, so naturally I had positioned myself close enough to Clam from where I was likely to hear the entire conversation that followed.

'Clam! Thank God, I've finally got hold of you! 'It's Police Captain David Orr in Darwin.'

'Oh, g'day there David, what on earth's happened that you need to speak to me while I'm in Poland? I'm heading back to Australia from Warsaw today. Is that of any help?'

'Yes, probably. This news affects your colleague Thommo, as much as you.'

'Actually, he's sitting at the other end of the bar talking to his new girlfriend, so David, you'd best get this off your chest with me, first like.'

'OK. Mate, you'd better get back to Darwin asap. I've got a ninety-three-year-old Australian bloke in my lock-up. He reckons he's come all the way from Bruges to meet Thommo, and that he's dying, and that he calls himself The Diamond Whisperer ... whatever that means.

'He's also got an envelope for Thommo but will only hand it over to him in person. Apparently, that envelope contains officially autho-rised release documents for Thommo to take possession as the sole beneficiary of his ill-gotten lifetime fortune.'

'Mate, you're a pearl for rushing this info to us. Thanks heaps. We'll be on a plane within an hour destined for Singapore and then transferring to a Qantas flight to Darwin, which, if we're lucky should get us to Darwin in about sixteen hours.

'But David, whatever you do, don't let that old bugger die. He's the only person alive who knows the exact whereabouts of the world's largest ever diamond theft... and who's the prime suspect for murdering more than thirty people over the past three decades.'

* * *

FOLLOWING an uneventful flight back to Darwin, we were ushered to The Diamond Whisperer's cell. All I got from him was a guttural, 'Don't know this individual, he can piss off.'

Those few words were sufficient proof to me that all along, Canberra really knew what they were doing. Their gamble, that if I could get close enough to our suspect, I would recognise him, but that he would have no idea who I was from my makeover, had paid off in spades.

As I was leaving the cell, I heard our man say to Clam, 'Well, well, we finally meet. You do know I've had an eye on you, yah black bastard; far too long, I should 'ave dealt with *you* years ago when I had the chance.'

That said, Clam simply smiled then walked out of the cell with his arm laid across my shoulder, leaving Thommo alone with our prisoner, their privacy guaranteed.

Two hours passed before Thommo called to Captain Orr to release him from that man's cell. Apparently, there was no emotional reaction from Thommo as he exited that cell; no hug, no handshake offered ... and moreover, no final words of apology or regret from his father!

No doubt that meeting had been a mortifying experience for Thommo, but being the professional he was, he extracted many details which would help to convict that felon of his many self-confessed thefts and senseless killings.

Regrettably, time saved him from public exposure and yet, he was probably welcomed with open arms when he finally landed in Hell.

* * *

About six weeks after returning from Europe, we received a disturbing intelligence communique from our partners in Bruges. Of the many items of potential evidence taken from the front office of the Swiss Bank where Thommo almost succeeded in capturing our felon, several fingerprints taken from magazine covers had matched those of "known people of interest".

Subsequent investigations uncovered the decayed bodies of four of those suspects; all had been shot in the head and were found at various locations in and round Amsterdam, Bruges and Warsaw.

A fifth more recent murder, the proprietor of two jewellery and gift shops located in Singapore was also brought to our attention; apparently that killing occurred simultaneously with the time The Diamond Whisperer was enroute to Australia.

Vale Archie; what a dope.

30

———————

Eighteen months later Joan and I married. We immediately adopted that lovely Polish girl, Jennie, who graciously accepted *Zarkas* as her new family name.

When we moved into our house, regrettably the previous owners forgot to take their ageing male cat with them. He too was adopted by us, but the first thing I purchased was an eight-week-old tri-colour Maine Coon kitten ... to keep the old bloke company.

I don't believe I'd ever really been so happy and content before in my life, except for one matter which tormented me; the recurring belief that I needed to satisfy my curiosity regarding that Japanese pilot.

Though my role with Canberra was officially over, Joan, Jenni and I always made a point of catching up with Clam, Leigh and Thommo for drinks and dinner whenever the three of them were in town.

On one such occasion, when the others were discussing the upcoming Test Match Cricket series between Australia and England, Clam said to me, quietly, 'mate, I'd be happy to arrange for you and Joan to visit Japan but now is not the time.

'The political situation over there's unstable and domestic resentment of Australia still exists, besides the radio activity situation from those two A-bombs the Yanks dropped on Japan is still problematic and probably will be so for several more years.

'So that you know, I've already given Leigh the job of digging around, so to speak, to see what he can find out about that Jap pilot. No point though trying to cajole anything from him, Richard, he's under instructions that he only discuss his findings with me.

'In the meantime, how about a trip to New Zealand? Everything'll be paid by Canberra as appreciation of services rendered. Nothing less than three weeks and it should be fantastic over there at this time of year. Of course you will not be on any sanctioned work, but should you need help of any kind, you know who to ask. Well, what do yah reckon?'

'Christ Almighty Clam, you don't have to do that,' I mumbled my reply.

'Yeah, mate, we do!' Clam replied firmly, putting an end to any further debate.

'Mind you, I'd obviously be most grateful if you can arrange that, so yes, I'll take you up on that kind offer. But let's keep it quiet; it'll be a beaut surprise for Joan.'

My mind was in overdrive. 'Hang on a sec Clam,' I quickly added, 'you do realise Joan'll need to receive authorisation for three weeks of holiday time. Would that be OK? And mate, what on earth should we do with Jennie, while we're away, like?'

'Don't you worry about the admin stuff,' Clam dived in, 'we'll take care of that. But the only way I can solve your concerns for young Jennie's welfare, is, well, you'll just have to take her with you! Simple!'

31

I'm into my nineties now and some would say I'm still a silly old
bastard. Maybe, but my mind is still sharp as a tack and physi-
cally I'm doing OK, still riding my mountain bike about twenty
kilometres every other day.

And, thanks to my wife and daughter, I've learnt to relax. Yet
somehow, life can still offer up a surprise or two.

One morning in early Spring, I rode to a favourite location beside
the Molonglo River. Just as I dismounted, a Nissan 4WD pulled up
beside me; that person could have parked anywhere, for this location
was clear everywhere within fifty metres.

I stood my bike against a viewing bench then turned to see who
had chosen to upset my equanimity. Facing me, not a metre away was
Clam. His next step was into my arms, enveloping me into a strong
hug. I returned that hug for I hadn't seen nor heard from my greatest
and dearest friend for several months.

'Good God mate, you still know how to frighten the bejesus out of
a bloke. I never heard you open your car door or walk up to me;
Christ Almighty, you could've given me a stroke.'

We sat side by side on the viewing bench, saying nothing for a
minute or so before Clam said, 'I promised that one day I'd teach you

how to that, but I'll have to renege; time's caught up with me and ... well, Richard, I'm dying; I've got a cancer on my brain, what's left of it.'

It wasn't the cold morning air which sent a shiver down my back. We all, I suspect, fear the day of our own passing, but to lose your best friend can also be paralysing. Eventually I muttered, 'How long have you got and who else have you told?'

'Well, let me put it this way, I won't be around when you step off. Apparently, my condition's inoperable and it's working overtime on destroying my grey matter: the experts reckon four or five weeks at best. I've only told you and I'd like you to keep it that way. But I want you to help me with something ...'

'Anything mate, you know that.'

'I want to be buried in my ancestral birthplace. Can you arrange that for me?'

'Of course. But when, and should I be contacting any of your folk in the meantime? Do you want a traditional back to earth funeral for example?

'I'll let you know all those details as soon as I've sorted out a few things.'

A much longer silence followed.

'There's something else I need to tell you,' Clam said softly, 'best it comes from me.'

We casually looked at each other, that being the cue for Clam to continue.

'Yesterday, I received some disturbing news from Canberra. Apparently, Leigh's father, Peter, most unexpectedly got most of his paintings back ... about a month ago.'

'That's good news surely? What's disturbing about that pray tell?'

'Every piece of his work was maliciously damaged, rendering them worthless ... and Peter has been murdered; just two days ago.'

'Good God, no!'

'There were witnesses ... and an arrest. Someone you should remember.'

'Who?'

'Wacław Kluczewski was recently released from jail for her involvement in trying to kill you, and for aiding and abetting that bastard Diamond Whisperer.'

'Shit! Does Leigh know about this?'

'Unfortunately, yes. Now, cop this: she's admitted to having organised Peter's murder ... on the basis that he and Leigh needed to be punished for identifying her husband via those sketches Leigh produced.

'Canberra will invite you to attend Peter's funeral, but you'll have to also represent this old blackfeller.'

* * *

"WE ONLY DANCE on this world for a short time" was one of Clam's favourite sayings, and he sure did that with style. So many great memories shared and such a gift to have him as my unconditionally trustworthy and fascinating friend.

THE END

AUTHOR'S EXPLANATORY NOTES

When researching this story, several matters arose which would regrettably prove difficult to substantiate. Yet, therein, surely lay the foundation of a novel.

However, it soon became evident to me that Warsaw was (and probably still is) an international hub for diamond processing and trading.

Coincidently or not, historically, Warsaw also underwent a period when several resident Royalties and rich businessmen were somehow separated from their rightful property, and despite expansive efforts to locate their precious diamonds, that has not happened ... and may never happen.

Yet somehow a mysterious name, *The Diamond Whisperer*, had seeped into the lexicon of European diamond trading circles. It was rumoured that a ruthless operator was somehow at play.

That person seemed able to gain information "on nothing but the faintest whisper" about the whereabouts, size and movement of diamond transfers around the globe, including to and from Australia.

Some folk speculated that so many successful thefts meant only one thing: that each theft had to involve an insider, yet no suspects surfaced, and the thefts continued. Given the best of my research, nobody has ever located those stolen jewels. Nor had Peter's artworks "ever seen the legitimate light of day since surrendering them to the supposed safe keeping in a Swiss Bank ... until they surfaced, ruined, a few days before Peter's murder."

* * *

Somebody must have known The Diamond Whisperer.

Yet, he was never apprehended; he did however eventually surrender to the Australian Police in Darwin.

Many folks who either "just innocently crossed his path", or who tried to circumvent his daringly outrageous thefts and his methods of evasion, were ruthlessly murdered. Theft investigations officers were convinced he was maniacally obsessed that those persons had the ability to recognize him ... and therefore they had to be eliminated if his chosen deranged lifestyle was to survive.

Those murders were not confined to Europe. At least thirteen "executions" were carried out in Australia at his behest by an equally demented, former Vietnamese soldier and his wife. You can read all about that in my fourth novel, *God Only knows When;* an insight into the criminal underbelly of rural Australia. To learn more, please visit my website: www.trevortuckerpublishing.com.au.

* * *

It is a fact that on the third of March 1942, a WW2 Japanese pilot flying a Zero fighter bomber, shot down a Douglas DC-3 Dakota not long after it had taken off from Broome. Throughout Australia, that piece of our history seems to have been forgotten; very little is known about what became of the Dakota and alarmingly, that so few people knew about a precious cargo having been on board.

Some commentary speculated that the Americans destroyed that plane to minimise evidence which could prove embarrassing to them. However, a more logical outcome is that literally, time and tide took care of that political conundrum.

Also, very little is known about those killed in the crash landing ... were they Australians, Americans, private citizens, politicians or senior militia?

Furthermore, very little is recorded about what attempts were made by the then Australian Government to find and arrest those who located and took possession (and then disappeared) with that cargo, which was after all, supposed to be in our safe hands once that Dakota crossed the coast of Australia. That precious cargo was a pragmatic investment by several European countries to commence infrastructure reparation works once Adolf Hitler was eliminated.

That Japanese Zero referred to was part of the assets belonging to a Japanese aircraft carrier which was officially observed navigating the Torres Straits on that fateful day.

Here I divert slightly. You may recall that a fictitious character, Ronnie Burgess, a resident of New Guinea, may well have been a real character, and bless him, would have been well placed to have been an important person working for the Australian Defence forces as a coastline spotter of enemy shipping movements.

But why was it 'that a **lone** Zero" was initially reported, and who was the pilot?

The reality was that that plane was part of a three-plane Zero formation, led by Lieutenant Zenjiro Miyano. Miyano was a highly regarded Japanese fighter pilot and was considered one of the best leaders produced by the Imperial Japanese Navy Air Force. On that fateful day, Miyano no doubt took it upon himself to shoot down that Dakota; an easy kill to add to his growing list of victories [He later went on to claim sixteen victories before being killed in action at Guadalcanal.]

Could that action have been pre-arranged between The Diamond Whisperer and Miyano? It would have been possible because our thief, a mild-mannered gentleman working for a Swiss Bank would have been able to not only learn of the intended international transfer of diamonds, but to have even assembled that near priceless package.

Furthermore, it is not out of the question such "a highly regarded and trusted individual" would learn not only about the Dakota's intended route over Australia, but also the date and time at which it would most likely attempt to leave Broome.

Interestingly, prior to the commencement of WW2, Miyano had spent time touring Europe. He could have met The Diamond Whisperer when he became a client of that Swiss Bank and become friends as "common soldiers of fortune."

It was reliably reported a portion of that diamond consignment was presented to the Broome police as evidence that the diamonds had all been found. However, there is no record (that I could locate) detailing exactly where that "sample" ended up, though some conjectured it was given as a reward to those who rescued the survivors after the Dakota's crash landing.

As unlikely as that is, it still begs the question "what really happened to the balance of those diamonds and how did The Diamond Whisperer get his hands on them?'

For example, did Miyano play a pivotal role in somehow retrieving those diamonds, for, and on behalf of The Diamond Whisperer before he was killed in action?

It's my belief that Thommo could somehow have teased the answer to that question from his father; it then becoming an integral part of his father's confession. But that's another story.

* * *

You might be interested to learn, as I was, about Swiss Banks; they do by necessity play a significant role in this novel.

For example, they not only accept (huge) cash deposits, but just about anything from gold bullion to diamonds (uncut or otherwise) … and, even soil samples for prospecting companies, or for individual prospectors.

Historically, no local or international authority was ever given permission to inspect "the material contents" of a Swiss Bank account, regardless of any excuse for wanting to do so. Apparently, that's because "it would potentially jeopardise Switzerland's political neutrality."

Since the end of WW2, that has marginally changed. Nevertheless, Swiss Banks still do not currently allow inspection of deposits that exceed US $150k.

Still, Swiss Banks offer high security, "relatively low fees" and are not subject to tax … which of course make them an attractive investment for certain "players".

The visible workplaces of Swiss Banks (those accessible from the street) are a front only. All physical deposits are stored (usually underground) in high security facilities, and those locations are known by very few people.

And, when those people pass away, their replacement seldom learn those locations as part of their induction, in some cases, never. Spare a thought about the poor buggers who work at those storage locations; what would be the consequences of breaching in-house security protocols?

Also, apparently, there is a significant protocol surrounding proof of identity of all depositors … and believe it or not, of the suitability of the person, or business, nominated as the beneficiary, *before* a deposit will be accepted! Go figure.

Yet, in fact, herein was a significant portion of the material which I needed to "massage" into a convincing story.

* * *

My assumption that those stolen European diamonds might never be found can be challenged. It has been suggested to me that the Diamond Whisperer may have found it quite easy to dispose of them, not in a literal sense, but in their transformation to very expensive works of art to be subsequently sold on the Black Market. The diamond trade is, and always has been, one of secrecy.

* * *

Throughout this story I've referred to either "our man in Canberra" or, simply, "Canberra". That person first makes an appearance in my previous novel, "God Only Knows When". My character is fictitious, though in reality there is a need to maintain confidentiality of the real-life director: hence the less said about that person and their over-arching responsibilities, the better.

* * *

Do you believe in coincidence, e.g. of two related events occurring on the same date, <u>though separated by eighty years</u>? Consider the odds: while Australians were celebrating the end of WW2 against the Japanese, that on the 15th of August 2025, I wrote **THE END** to this novel.

ACKNOWLEDGMENTS

Leigh Nation. Barber extraordinaire. Mate, thanks for your inspiration and wisdom that allowed me to link the underbelly of international diamond racketeering with an incredible indigenous character from one of my previous novels. I hope you approve.

Tony Park. Friend, master storyteller and creator of twenty-three amazing African based novels. Thanks for your invaluable help in ensuring all my novels now display the AUSTRALIAN MADE logo.

Anne Edwards. Retired bank manager, friend, and breeder of Banded Galway cattle. Thanks for helping unravel an awkward and critical part of this story by triggering an imaginary insight into the role played by Swiss Banks.

Jamie Robinson. Website developer extraordinaire and friend. Thanks, mate, for your timely recommendations, planning and attention to detail.

Andrzej Soszynski. The Honourable Consul General for the Republic of Poland in Victoria. Thanks so much for your contribution enhancing the authenticity of typical (though fictitious) Polish person's names and place names used throughout this novel.

Callum Tucker. My incredible son; thanks for your tolerance of my "intense periods of isolation" and for your amazing, insightful support.

Yve Versteegen. Proofreader extraordinaire. Thanks again for your *incredible* eye for detecting and correcting my inadvertent grammatical errors.

ABOUT THE AUTHOR

Inspired by the joy and intense satisfaction of writing my first six books. Aussie Anecdotes, A Sense of Justice, God Only Knows When, and Wonnangatta, I embarked on my seventh authorial adventure, The Diamond Whisperer.

Over the years I've formed the belief that writing is a most satisfying outlet for creativity ... both challenging and relaxing. However, writing is not just escapism, but rather the compulsion of a glorious illness which I refer to as The Dreamer's Disease.

Having retired from the oil and gas industry, my other interests have since included (whenever possible) spending time with my kids, and grandkids, fishing, bike riding, watching Test cricket and AFL/AFLW footy and listening to classical music ... but most of all, enjoying the life-changing experiences of travelling the world.

If you enjoyed reading The Diamond Whisperer, please consider my previous books outlined on the pages that follow.

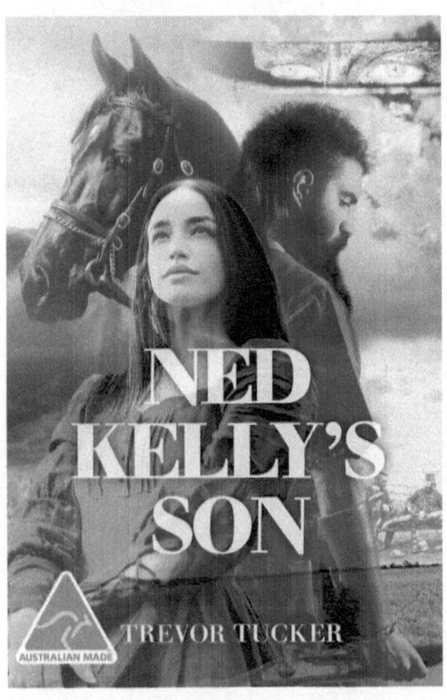

Ned Kelly's Son
By Trevor Tucker

Beautiful, headstrong Orla O'Meara escapes persecution in 19th century Ireland to start a new life in the wild colony of Victoria, Australia.

There she meets the continent's most notorious bushranger, Ned Kelly and a brief, passionate relationship results in the birth of the outlaw's unknown son, Niall.

After Ned's violent death, Orla and her son have to learn to survive in this tough, unforgiving land. Their travels, together with a faithful Waler horse named Boss Boy, take them throughout Australia and bring them up against criminals, goldminers, loggers and the police.

Ned Kelly's Son is a sweeping saga, following mother and son and the family's descendants through Australia's transition from a collection of colonies to a nation born during the Boer War, in which Niall serves.

The Kellys fight injustice and champion the rights of aboriginal people through a hundred years of struggle, poverty, romance, wealth, pain and redemption.

The Stolen Maps
By Trevor Tucker

It is 1519 and two intrepid Portuguese seafarers set off on separate missions to different parts of the globe. Their journeys intersect with the European discovery of 'The Great South Land'.

Manny Perez, young and adventurous, and Cristo de Mendonça an older, experienced naval officer, become friends and agree to map the east coast of this wild continent, unknown to white people.

Danger and death await on land and sea as the explorers make contact with the indigenous people of this strange new place, and face the worst that nature can hurl at their ships.

Lost, re-drawn, then stolen, Manny and Cristo's precious maps become a treasure sought after in a race between empires.

Heroism, tragedy, romance and intrigue reverberate all the way through history, leading to the discovery of a secret lying buried beneath modern Australia's coastal sands.

God Only Knows When
By Trevor Tucker

Failed farmer Andy Stevens' life takes a turn for the better when he meets and marries Sydney barrister Beth Carmichael, but before they can settle into their new life the couple is recruited by the Federal Government as Livestock Theft Investigation officers.

Livestock theft – sheep and cattle rustling – is the thriving but little-known sinister underbelly of Australian rural life.

Along with their leader, Beau, a no-nonsense former drover, two high-flying young army officers and an aboriginal investigator, the team tackle stock theft head-on and commence a hunt for a killer who is preying on Australian farmers and taking their land.

The criminal web they uncover is far reaching and diverse, encompassing native bird and reptile smuggling, counterfeiting and even a fine-art racket dating back to the Second World War.

Even as their successes mount, Andy, Beth and their teammates have to watch their backs. Who knows who is really pulling the strings?

Reader review: "A thoroughly enjoyable read. Trevor has embraced a significant topic which is often overlooked and seldom, if ever, understood by those who do not live in regional Australia."

A Sense of Justice
By Trevor Tucker

Two young Englishmen, Harry Taylor, a minor felon, and Patrick Galbraith, a navy marine lieutenant serving on the final convict transport ship bound for Australia in 1867, become friends on the voyage.

Harry and Patrick both end up in Trial Bay Prison on the north coast of New South Wales.

In return for good behaviour, an early release allows them to explore the hinterland. Opportunity knocks when the pair have a violent run-in with bushrangers and land a windfall beyond their wildest dreams.

But their newfound wealth also haunts their adventurous lives, through a series of pivotal encounters with cattle thieves, murderers, colourful figures of the colony's racing and farming industries, and a young Aboriginal woman.

Harry and Patrick both find love in the arms of beautiful women, but their good fortune comes under threat when a ghost from their past emerges.

Wonnangatta
By Trevor Tucker

An abandoned five-year-old English boy, Leon, is rescued by a compassionate neighbouring family who adopt Leon and move with him to Australia for a better life in 1903.

Rocky, a relative of the family already in Australia, allows them to reside in his majestic country homestead, near Wangaratta in Victoria. Rocky clearly has considerable wealth, though it soon becomes clear he didn't earn it through hard work.

Leon embraces farming and rural life in the wild colony, but unbeknown to him, he is being groomed for bigger, murkier things.

When two men are murdered on a remote cattle station, Rocky, Leon and Adam, an aboriginal man, go in search of the killer. In the process they become embroiled in cattle theft, fraud and more death.

Wonnangatta is a sweeping saga of mystery, romance and intrigue played out against the raw beauty of the Australian bush.